"Let me do that for you."

Jade spun around. She hadn't heard him come into the kitchen behind her, and she didn't like the subtle, knowing smile on his lips.

She smiled thinly in return, handed him the wine and moved several steps away, crossing her arms over her chest. "Please," she murmured.

She felt hot and feverish all over again as she watched his fingers, watched his expertise as he dealt with the wine and the glasses. He handed her one, and she took a long swallow. The wine was very good; it was bottled courage.

What was she so nervous about? It was just dinner. And then . . . ? Lord, she had every right to be nervous! But for all Jeff's temper and the maddening mockery of his smile, there were few men with his sensitivity.

It was now or never.

Dear Reader,

When two people fall in love, the world is suddenly new and exciting, and it's that same excitement we bring to you in Silhouette Intimate Moments. These are stories with scope, with grandeur. These characters lead the lives we all dream of, and everything they do reflects the wonder of being in love.

Longer and more sensuous than most romances, Silhouette Intimate Moments novels take you away from everyday life and let you share the magic of love. Adventure, glamour, drama, even suspense— these are the passwords that let you into a world where love has a power beyond the ordinary, where the best authors in the field today create stories of love and commitment that will stay with you always.

In coming months look for novels by your favorite authors: Maura Seger, Parris Afton Bonds, Elizabeth Lowell and Erin St. Claire, to name just a few. And whenever you buy books, look for all the Silhouette Intimate Moments, love stories *for* today's women *by* today's women.

Leslie J. Wainger
Senior Editor
Silhouette Books

IMRL-7/85

Heather Graham Pozzessere

The Game of Love

Silhouette Intimate Moments

Published by Silhouette Books New York

America's Publisher of Contemporary Romance

SILHOUETTE BOOKS
300 East 42nd St., New York, N.Y. 10017

Copyright © 1986 by Heather Graham Pozzessere

ISBN: 0-373-07165-5

First Silhouette Books printing November 1986

America's Publisher of Contemporary Romance

Printed in the U.S.A.

HEATHER GRAHAM POZZESSERE

considers herself lucky to live in Florida, where she can indulge her love of water sports, like swimming and boating, year-round. Her background includes stints as a model, actress and bartender. She was once actually tied to the railroad tracks to garner publicity for the dinner theater where she was acting. Now she's a full-time wife, mother of four and, of course, a writer of historical and contemporary romances.

Prologue

And stri—ke three! Yessirree, you heard the ump, folks! Strike three it is; the World Series goes to the Sox in a nutshell, Martin bringing them to glory straight off the pitcher's mound!''

The subdued sound of a television greeted Jeff as he entered his darkened town house. He shook his head, frowning as he quietly closed the door, slipped out of his coat and dusted the snow from it. It was a fierce night, even for Chicago, howling with wind, and bitter with cold.

There was a faint glow coming from the living room; he walked down the hallway and stood in the doorway as his eyes adjusted to the light coming from the television set.

He tensed, watching the quick blur of images as they passed over the screen; the eleven o'clock nightly news was doing a series on local celebrities. Tonight

the piece was about *him*. Dirk Hagen, an old teammate and friend, was sitting on the sofa watching the
screen. He was as unaware of Jeff as Jeff was of him.

The sportscaster claimed that Jeffrey Martin was
one of the best pitchers alive, and went on to say that
it was a damned pity his career had been cut short by
a skiing accident.

Jeff winced—not because his career had been cut
short. He'd never felt that playing baseball was his
only option in life. But the newsreel did have the
power to hurt him, because it brought back memories.

He hadn't wanted to ski. He'd gone on the party
weekend because Diana had wanted to go. It hurt to
remember that. To remember the way she'd thrown
herself all over him while the cameras were rolling, and
walked out the moment the doctors said that he'd
never play baseball again. They'd said he'd be lucky
if he ever walked again.

But he could walk now. Two years of grinding
therapy had taught him to walk again, without a limp
most of the time.

And Diana...

There she was on the screen. A picture of their
wedding flashed onto the television, then one of their
leaving the hospital together when Ryan was born. The
commentator had been generous with praise that
night: he'd called Jeff the best pitcher ever; Diana he'd
described as possibly the most beautiful woman in the
world.

Well, that she was, Jeff thought dryly. And she sure
did like to see that her beauty was appreciated by all.

He strode across the room and snapped off the television, then went to the bar and poured himself a drink.

"Hell's fire, Jeffrey Martin!" Dirk complained. "I didn't hear you walk in."

Dirk was a sandy-haired, wiry athlete; it seemed strange to see him tense and on the edge of his seat.

Jeff chuckled softly. "Sorry, Dirk. Want a drink?"

"Yeah. Yeah, after that, I sure as hell do."

Jeff poured out a shot of bourbon for Dirk and handed it to him.

"Did Ryan wake up?" he asked.

"Nope. Haven't heard a word from him."

"Thanks for coming. I appreciate it."

"It was nothing," Dirk mumbled. Then he stared at Jeff curiously. "Well, uh, was everything all right?"

Jeff shrugged and took a long sip of bourbon, glad of the fire it sent through him. "Yeah, everything is okay. She was at a boat party with some Canadian players and had a few too many drinks. When she called me, she was practically incoherent. I was worried that she wouldn't get home okay. I found her..."

"And she was pretty messed up, huh?"

"Who knows with Diana? She's the ultimate actress. Anyway, I took her home, tucked her in and left.

Dirk stared at the blank television screen. The room was so quiet Jeff could hear the soft ticking of the mantle clock.

"Well, I sure as hell don't know why you do it!" Dirk suddenly exclaimed. "She cheated on you, and you gave her a chance. She left you, and you finally divorced her. Now, every time she's in a scrape, she gives you a call, and you pick up the pieces. I'll be damned if I know why!''

Jeff didn't respond to his friend's anger. He sipped his drink then said softly, "What am I supposed to do, Dirk? She's still Ryan's mother, and he adores her. I have to pick up the pieces when I can.''

"She's as wild as a cougar," Dirk muttered resentfully. "And as mean.''

"No, no she isn't,'' Jeff said slowly. "She's just absolutely careless of other people's feelings.''

"You still, uh, see her now and then?''

Jeff laughed easily. "Now and then, but then was a while ago.'' He grinned at his friend. "It's okay now. Because I don't care anymore. Seeing her is just like seeing any other woman.''

"Hmmph!'' Dirk snorted. He didn't like Diana. He'd been there when she'd walked out on Jeff.

"You should hate her," Dirk said.

"Well—'' Jeff took a seat on the couch, stretching his legs out before him "—I don't.''

"You're not bitter?''

"Sure, a little.'' His expression softened. "But she gave me Ryan, and he's the best thing in my life.''

Dirk gazed over at Jeff Martin and smiled. Jeff was six three, broad in the shoulders, lean, rugged and damned good-looking. He'd never needed to play ball to attract the opposite sex, and his charisma had enabled him to move quickly from the ball park to the TV screen as an announcer.

But he'd never cared much about the adulation. He'd always been a private man, fond of his home, of quiet, intimate gatherings. How he and Diana had gotten together in the first place was a mystery. How they'd stayed married for seven years was another puzzle. Dirk couldn't help feeling that the divorce was best for all concerned. Particularly since Jeff had gotten custody of his son. No one could love a kid more than Jeff Martin loved nine-year-old Ryan.

"Yeah, Ryan is a fine kid," Dirk said. The boy took after his old man, he decided, not in looks, but in personality.

"So what are you going to do?" Dirk demanded. "Spend the rest of your life in casual affairs while you pick up Diana every time she tries one of her ploys?"

Jeff grinned. "Nope."

"Well, that's what you did tonight."

"I won't be doing it again."

"Oh, yeah. And why not?"

"I'm moving. To Miami."

"Miami! You're going to leave Chicago for Miami?"

Dirk felt that Chicago was the height of sophistication—and that any other place was simply uncivilized.

"Yeah." Jeff smiled slowly, lifting his drink. "I got a nice job offer from one of the network affiliates down there, and it sounded good to me. Palm trees, sunshine, sailing—"

"Hmm. And girls in bikinis."

The move was starting to sound better to Dirk. But then he sobered. "And a new life, huh?"

Jeff stood up and walked to the window. He watched as the snow beat against the panes. There was a lot of pain still, and a lot of bitterness for him here in Chicago. And it would probably be the best thing in the world for Diana to realize that if she wanted her own life, she had to live it—by herself.

He lifted his glass to Dirk, and to his own reflection in the windowpane.

"Yep. A new life."

Chapter 1

Jade had barely turned onto Ponce when she realized that Sean's folder was still on the passenger seat of her old Corvette.

"Damn," she swore softly, frustrated. It had been one of those "Murphy's Law" mornings: every little thing that could go wrong had. She'd forgotten to put Sean's gym clothes in the dryer, every pair of panty hose she owned had runs, the mayonnaise had turned and she'd somehow managed to char bacon in a microwave!

And now this! She'd have to turn around and go back to school. Sean's math teacher took no excuses for incomplete homework.

She shook her head a little woefully. Sean had a bad enough time in math without being marked down for no homework.

Traffic was ridiculously heavy on Ponce that morning. She couldn't get anyone to let her into the left lane to make a turn. The Metrorail went screeching by on her right and she jumped, the system had been in for ages, but the sound still made her certain that Russian SST's were attacking.

She gritted her teeth, flicked on her blinker and swore again. "Miami has the rudest damned drivers in the world."

When the light had changed three times and she was still caught in the right lane, Jade rolled down her window. There was a young man in the car at her left, and she beeped to get his attention. He was snapping his fingers to the rhythm of a rock song that seemed to be shaking the entire body of his classic Chevy.

"Hey!" she called out. He couldn't possibly hear her, so she beeped again. At last he looked her way and gave her a wide smile.

"Hi!" he said brightly.

"Can I get over when the light changes, please?"

"Sure. Nice car."

"Thanks."

"What's your name?"

Jade couldn't help smiling in amusement. The kid was cute. He had nice shaggy brown hair, dark eyes and a great smile. Probably a sophomore, she decided, and definitely University of Miami—he had bumper stickers promoting the Hurricanes all over the car.

She was surprised that he was flirting with her. She must be looking better than she'd imagined this morning if this young thing was trying to pick her up.

"Jade," she replied, shouting a bit over the sound of their motors and the music.

"Jade. Neat name. Want to meet for lunch?" He grinned.

Jade laughed, shaking her head.

"I'm too old!"

"Too old for what? Even my grandparents eat lunch."

She shook her head, still smiling. The light changed, and he gallantly allowed her to speed ahead of him.

Her smile slowly faded as she faced a new traffic jam in the turn lane. Jade groaned. It was going to take time before she could actually make her left.

She rolled up her window and turned on the air conditioning. It was November, but the weather was still miserably hot. The day was humid and the temperature was nearly ninety.

"I'll wilt before I ever get to the office," she muttered. Aggravated, she switched on her radio. The car began to cool. She leaned back and tried to relax. When she opened her eyes again, she saw the velvet green of the grass along the median and the pretty vines growing up the Metrorail support. The sky was a dazzling blue, and to her right, palm fronds waved pleasantly in the subtle breeze.

She glanced fleetingly at her reflection in the rearview mirror. What had the young man seen? She was wearing a modicum of makeup—just lipstick and a dash of mascara. She grimaced. Maybe it was her hair. There was a lot of it, and the tawny strands were very windblown at the moment. Maybe it looked like a stylish modern cut from a distance.

The light changed. She inched forward. Then, miracle of miracles, the cars ahead of her began to move. She might—just might—get her chance to make that left.

There was something big coming...a Lincoln? A Caddy? She wasn't sure. But the light switched to yellow. In seconds, she made up her mind. She gunned the Corvette, certain that the oncoming car would stop for the changing light.

But just as she turned, the flow of traffic through the intersection stopped, and she had to slam on her brakes. "Oh, hell..." she began.

And then before she could finish her exclamation of annoyance, the Corvette jerked and shuddered—and a long scraping sound filled her ears.

"No! Oh, no! That damned idiot!" she wailed aloud.

The big car hadn't stopped. It was now attached to her rear bumper. And there was a man stepping out of it—a man as big as the damned car. He was six three if he was an inch, broad shouldered, well muscled and trim. He was dressed in a handsomely tailored three-piece pin-striped suit.

Some high-tech executive with money, she thought furiously, in such a hurry to make more money that he can't even keep his eye on traffic.

As he approached, she realized he looked furious. A lock of dark chestnut hair had fallen over his forehead and mirrored sunglasses covered his eyes, but his anger was easy to read nonetheless. His strides were long, his mouth was grim and his chin had a belligerent cast to it.

How dared he look like that! she thought, and without pausing to consider her action, she wrenched her own door open, ready to fly into battle.

"You ass!" a deep male voice accosted her angrily. "You could have killed yourself! Thank God I was able to stop when I did! You could have been a mangled corpse in that sardine can!"

"Me!" Jade shrilled in return. She would never admit it, but the Corvette was a bit of a sardine can. All of a sudden she didn't seem to be able to extricate her long legs from the low-slung seat. "Sir, did you purchase your driver's license at Sears? Red lights mean that you're supposed to stop!"

"It was yellow!"

"Like hell it was!" Oh, she was angry. Righteously angry. He was leaning over the Corvette now, and horns were blaring everywhere. She tried again to get out of the car. Unfortunately, the high heel of her shoe caught in the doorframe and she pitched right into her adversary.

Strong hands caught her shoulders, steadying her. She wrenched herself out of his grip.

"You hit me, you fool!" she retorted. "Everyone knows that you are at fault when you hit from the rear—"

"I had the right-of-way! You bolted out in front of me!"

"You just wait till the police get here. They'll give you the ticket—you'll see!"

He put his hands on his hips, oblivious to all the honking around them. He cocked his head slightly, and suddenly he smiled, as if he were amused with the situation, though in heaven's name, Jade couldn't imagine why."

"Are you all right?" he asked her.

"What?"

"You weren't hurt?"

"No," she mumbled, lowering her head slightly in confusion. He'd made such an abrupt about-face.

"Then if your car is still driveable, I suggest we get in and do just that—drive. I assure you that if we wait for the police, you'll get the ticket."

"What?" Jade asked, fuming all over again. "Oh, no! You're not getting out of this one!" She spun around, stiffening her shoulders in determination. That determination only intensified when she realized that his car barely had a dented fender.

The whole right rear end of hers was smashed in.

"No way," she repeated grimly, facing him again and wishing she could snatch the sunglasses from his face. Her eyes roamed over the length of his form again. His suit had a subtle elegance and was tailored to enhance the fine structure of his body. It was obviously very expensive. Like his car. Like his sunglasses. Like the after-shave that wafted pleasantly from him.

"Your insurance rate can go up because of this accident—not mine!" she told him, and quite suddenly, and annoyingly, she felt a little like crying. Her life wasn't so hard, no harder than that of a good many people doing their best to get by, but it would be so nice not to have to worry about every little setback.

He wouldn't have to worry. Not this man. So they raised his auto insurance. Big deal. He probably wouldn't even notice.

Unfortunately, Jade did have to worry. To make matters worse, she was going to be so late that Mr. Harrison would decide that if she couldn't even arrive at an appointment on time, how could she ever sell his house?

The stranger threw his hands up in the air suddenly and laughed. "Okay, lady, have it your way. We'll wait for the police. I'm sure someone will be along any moment."

He sat on the hood of her Corvette, casually folding his arms over his chest.

"Get off my car!" Jade began, but she didn't have a chance to press the point, because she heard a police siren then, and a second later a City of Miami patrol car was winding its way through the traffic to reach them.

"Now," Jade warned smugly, "we'll see who was at fault here."

He smiled enigmatically.

"Too bad you're such an irrational female. I might have bought you coffee while we had a mechanic check the damage to your car."

"What!" Jade eyed him again, then laughed dryly. What was this guy? Some kind of an overconfident jock dressed up in a business suit?

Yes, exactly, she decided. His size and build lent credence to her guess as did his slightly long hair and lazy smile. He'd probably played college football and picked up all the cheerleaders. And now he was grown up and working in an office, picking up his secretary instead, keeping muscled and trim at some spa. Maybe he was even married, but that wouldn't bother him too much. He was good-looking, affluent and had that sexual mystique certain men seemed to radiate. He was so confident of his appeal that he thought he would be able to buy her off with a cup of coffee.

Oh, did he deserve a ticket!

"What a shame," she retorted sarcastically. "But I don't drink coffee, anyway. We'll just have to speak to the nice officer coming our way."

"Fine," he said pleasantly. "I'll even let you start."

The officer was young and mustachioed and very pleasant.

"What happened here?" he asked with a sigh, studying the positions of the cars and Jade's driver's license as she drew it out of her purse.

"This gentleman ran a red light and hit me," Jade said sweetly.

"Officer, the light was yellow. This young lady streaked out right in front of me." With a nice smile, the jock slipped his hand into an inner pocket, produced a handsome leather wallet and extracted his license.

"Hmm." The officer removed his cap and walked carefully around the cars. Horns were still blaring. "Oh, cut it out," he mumbled to no one in particular.

He stared down at the licenses and up at the two of them. Then, to Jade's utter amazement, a smile lit his features.

"You're Jeffrey Martin? *The* Jeffrey Martin?"

The man laughed easily. "Well, I am Jeffrey Martin. Whether I'm 'the' or not is up for grabs."

"Oh, wow! I watched you for years! Religiously. Boy, were you great. I'd heard you were coming down here to work. Wow! Can I have your autograph?"

"Sure. Would you like it on a ticket, or on a piece of paper?"

The young officer started laughing as if there were some great joke between the two of them.

"Just paper, sir."

"Just paper!" Jade exploded. "But he hit me—"

The officer removed his cap and scratched his head, gazing at Jade apologetically. "I'm sorry, I'm afraid you get the ticket. You're out in the middle of the intersection."

"What?"

By that time the jock—*the* Jeffrey Martin, whoever he was—was scribbling away on a piece of miniature memo pad snatched from his inner pocket. He didn't look up. "I'm willing to forget the whole thing. You don't really have to give her a ticket, do you?"

Jeffrey Martin looked up and smiled very smugly at Jade. "There's really no need to involve the insurance companies then."

"Well, Mr. Martin," the officer said, "your car is damaged—"

"A scratch on the bumper. It's nothing."

"Well, my rear end is wrecked!" Jade wailed, still incredulous. "And it was your fault! Officer, don't you see—"

"I'd say your rear end will be just fine," Jeffrey Martin replied smoothly, pulling his glasses idly from his face.

She saw his eyes. They were blue, a sky blue, and they held a look of innuendo and amusement that almost made her slam her fists against her own car in frustration. She couldn't believe this. She just couldn't believe it.

"You can keep your opinion of my rear end to yourself!"

He arched his brows innocently. "The car really isn't badly damaged."

"I'll leave you two to settle this," the officer said. "Just move the cars. No ticket, Mrs. McLane. Please be more careful in the future. Mr. Martin, thank you. Thanks a lot. I can't wait to tell my kids and the wife!"

To Jade's total exasperation, that was it. The officer walked back to his car.

She glanced at Jeffrey Martin just in time to see him slip his sunglasses back on. The amusement in his striking eyes was no longer visible, but there was still an irritatingly smug smile on his lips.

"Do you drink tea instead of coffee?" he asked her.

"Arrgh!" The sound escaped without her permission, as did a tangle of oaths that didn't affect him in the least.

"Hey!" he warned her, sliding from the hood of her car. "You'd better learn to be careful. This can be a rough city. Some people will shoot you just for yelling from a car. I take it tea is out, huh? Well, then, if you'll excuse me, I've got to get to work."

And just like that, he walked past her. She was left to stare after him in utter amazement.

"Hey, lady! Move it!" one irate motorist screamed.

"Mama mia, stupida!" someone else joined in.

"Oh, stuff it," Jade muttered, but she crawled back beneath the wheel of her injured Corvette. A moment later she was hurrying away from the scene of the accident.

All the way down to Sunset, she swore wrathfully at Jeffrey Martin. She raved about men in general. She vowed to hang Sean upside down by his thumbs for forgetting his folder and causing the entire mess to begin with.

But then it wasn't really Sean's fault, and she knew it. She had been running late this morning even before she'd noticed the forgotten math assignment. She had to calm down and forget the accident, get Sean's folder to him and hope that Mr. Harrison would still be waiting.

And then she had to pray that she could afford the repairs to the Corvette. The car was fifteen years old, and she'd hoped to get at least another year's use out of it. She had always taken such good care of it.

She parked outside the school and hurried down the hall to Sean's homeroom class. She didn't want to interrupt his teacher, and so she stood in the doorway for a moment until Sean noticed her. His teacher saw her at the same time and nodded permission for Sean to meet her in the hallway.

Her tension eased somewhat as she watched him approach. Sean, she thought, was the one thing she had done right. At nine, he was tall and lean and handsome with beautiful crystal green eyes and shaggy blond hair. He was polite, easygoing and popular among his classmates. He also had an uncanny aptitude for sports, something that had frightened Jade ever since his father's death. She knew, though, that she couldn't keep a child from playing. Each time he took to the sports field, she choked back her feelings and displayed a plastic smile.

"Ah, Mom, thanks," he said, taking the folder from her. She smiled and tousled his hair while he looked at her searchingly. "You're going to be late, aren't you? For Mr. Harrison."

Sean was more aware of finances than a little boy should have to be, Jade thought. "I'm a little late. But it isn't your fault. Some fool smacked into my car."

"The Corvette?"

"It's the only car I have, kiddo."

"Can it be fixed?"

"Oh, yeah. It still runs. Listen, get back into class, okay?"

He nodded. "Thanks again. Oh, Mom, don't forget. It's your day."

"My day for what?"

"Practice. Little League. Remember? Mrs. Hodges drives the car pool Thursday; your day is Tuesday."

She stiffened; she couldn't help it. But she put her plastic smile into place and said, "I won't forget."

He scampered back into class. A minute later Jade was at her car, staring at the damage. She knew it was childish, but she kicked the tire, anyway.

"Damned pin-striped irresponsible macho cheat," she muttered. Oh. She felt sick. Here she was with a badly dented car while he had driven away with a scratched bumper.

Jake took a deep breath and fought for control. She couldn't change the events of the morning, so she might as well put them behind her. If she didn't get to the office soon, she would miss Mr. Harrison and make a disaster out of the afternoon, too.

Unfortunately, once she was behind the wheel again, she found she couldn't forget the episode. She talked aloud to the absent Jeffrey Martin.

"I hope your bumper falls off. I hope you get stuck in your office elevator. I hope your wife has an affair with her tennis instructor."

She decided not to go the way she had come and drove north through Coconut Grove instead. There, great banyan trees spread their branches over the road, and the landscape was rich with private homes and thick foliage. There was something soothing about the trees, about the shadows, about the image of a rich tropical jungle of flowers and mangrove roots, and the knowledge that the bay glittered just beyond the land to the right. Coconut Grove was the oldest section of Miami. Its central area, Main Street, had changed with the times, and she smiled to think of it. When she was eighteen, the Grove had been a haven for flower children. Incense had filled the streets, and Nehru jackets were plentiful in the park. Nowadays, the shops were all very chic and very expensive. But sidewalk cafés still lined the streets, and the kids still came, because there was something a little magical about the Grove, no matter how it changed.

Jade felt as if she could drive forever. With the radio on and the air conditioning emitting cool blasts of air, she wanted the road to go on indefinitely.

All too soon, she had to turn on to LeJeune and head back to Ponce. It was time to face her office and reality.

And a car that needed to be fixed, her appointment with Mr. Harrison and an early day—since she was car-pool mother.

"Oh, Sean," she said aloud, frowning. "Why couldn't you have been a brilliant mathematician instead of a star pitcher? And who the hell is Jeffrey Martin, anyway?''

Why had the cop fallen all over the man? Jade was certain that he wasn't an actor or a rock star. She would have recognized him, or at least his name. But then who was he?''

The man who wrecked my car and got away with it, she answered grimly.

Before she could give the matter more thought, she had reached the little office marked Harvin Realty. She could see Mr. Harrison's white Mercedes parked outside.

Quickly, she put several quarters into the meter, absently straightened her hair and made her way through the front door to the room that served as both her office and the reception area.

It was a nice room; she was proud of it. She had decorated it herself with plush beige carpeting and furniture she had found in antique shops and had restored herself. The windowpanes were stained glass; the coffee table was cherrywood, just like her desk. She had always felt that the antiques created an atmosphere where prospective clients would feel comfortable.

Jade barely noticed the room now. Her eyes went directly to the dignified, white-haired man sitting in front of her boss, Sandy Harvin.

"Mr. Harrison, I'm so sorry I'm late. I—"

"Oh, traffic." Mr. Harrison waved a hand in the air. "Quite all right. Sandy and I have been chatting. 'Bout the old times, mostly. Don't worry, Jade. I wouldn't trust The Grange to anyone but you. If you've got your contract ready, I'll just sign it now and be on my way.''

A sweeping sensation of gratitude filled Jade at these words. After the morning she had endured, she felt ridiculously like crying, or throwing herself at the old man's feet and swearing undying devotion.

She managed not to do anything so foolish. She did take his hand. ''Thank you. Thank you very much, Mr. Harrison. I'll do my absolute best to find a buyer who will make you happy.''

Harrison shrugged. ''Well, the market is tough right now. I'm not expecting miracles.''

Jade glanced at Sandy Harvin over Mr. Harrison's head. Her boss's shrug told her not to look a gift horse in the mouth.

Jade sat down with Mr. Harrison, and half an hour later she had all the information she needed for the listing. She also had his signature on the all important contract.

''I'm not living there anymore,'' Mr. Harrison told her. ''The place is just too much for me. Too big. Too many memories.''

Jade cleared her throat. ''I know what you mean,'' she said softly.

Ted Harrison had been a modern pioneer, coming to South Florida as a teenager in 1923. He and his wife, Melissa, had worked and struggled together. Together they had built the mansion that he called The Grange. Melissa had been dead for a year now, and Ted had decided that he didn't want to live in their dreamworld without her.

Jade had grown up just across the road from the two-acre waterfront spread, and she'd known the

Harrisons all her life. She was certain that was why
Ted was letting her sell his home. She was grateful; the
asking price was two million. The commission could
keep the wolf from her door for a long time.

"So how are you doing with your own place,
Jade?" Ted Harrison asked politely as he handed her
the keys to The Grange.

She smiled at him and gave a little shrug. "You
know how old places are. Something is always falling
apart."

He nodded sympathetically. "But you want to hang
on to it?"

Jade hesitated. "Yes, yes I do. The house was built
in 1925, you know. And there aren't many of those
original homes left down here anymore. And besides,
if—"

Ted Harrison laughed. "If you sold 'as is,' you
wouldn't get much of a price. Then some developer
would come in, turn it around, modernize and make
a fortune. No, you hang on to that house of yours,
young lady. One day it just might be the key to getting Sean through college. How's the boy?"

"Fine, thanks. Still awful in math, still great on the
field."

"Well, don't you worry too much about him.
Everybody's got a yen for something, and you've got
to go with that yen."

He stood, still tall and proud and straight for all his
seventy-five years. He placed a hand briefly on the top
of her head. "His daddy's accident was a fluke, you
know. The boy's gotta run; it's in his blood. And he'll
be okay. The good Lord will see to that."

She felt a tightness in her throat, but she smiled despite it. "I know. Thanks again, Mr. Harrison. The commission on your house will help me a lot."

"I hope so, Jade. I hope so."

He left the office. For several seconds, Jade just stared at the door. Then she realized that Sandy was watching her from the doorway to his inner office, and she turned to him.

His broad, fleshy face seemed to crinkle in a massive grin. "Well, Mrs. McLane, champagne lunch on me." He crossed the few feet between them and gave her a bone-crunching hug. "Wow! We're selling an historic landmark!"

Jade laughed and hugged him in return. "Oh, but Sandy! We've got to find a buyer. And times are tough out there right now."

"Ah, but The Grange isn't just any house."

"No, it needs someone with two million dollars to buy it."

"Tsk, tsk. Where is your sense of imagination and history? No matter how tight money is, you'll find the guy who wants The Grange. It's unique and special."

"Yes, it is. I wish I had two million dollars," Jade said. "I wish I had two thousand!" she added glumly. "Sandy, do you want to hear what happened this morning?" Indignantly, she went on to tell him about how she had been hit, but when she came to the part about the traffic cop's reaction, she couldn't remember the man's name. Sandy commiserated with her, offered to lend her money to fix her car, then reminded her that she was supposed to be showing the Hendersons an old Spanish home in North Gables.

Jade gasped, appalled that she was going to be late again, and sped out.

Sandy did take her out for a champagne lunch. A middle-aged bachelor, he was a bit of a fuddy-duddy, but Jade was often glad she had chosen to work for him instead of one of the real estate conglomerates. He was very kind to her; he understood the responsibilities of a single parent and never gave her a hard time about her hours or the emergencies that came along from time to time. Sandy had taken her in when she desperately needed work; he'd taught her all the ropes and became an important friend. Their lunch was very nice, and the champagne helped ease away the frustration of the morning's accident.

At three o'clock, just as she was about to leave for the day, the phone rang, and she made the mistake of answering it. It was the *Herald*, calling about a misprinted advertisement. By the time she had finished with the newspaper, she realized she was running late again.

"And on the first day of the Little League season!" she moaned to herself, grimacing wryly when Sandy came out of his office to tell her the time.

"Better get going," he counseled.

"Yes, I'd better."

It was a quarter to four before she picked up the boys, and by the time they reached the playing field things were already in full swing.

From far across the field, Lynn Fremont, the team "mother," waved to her. Jade smiled and waved back. The boys took off; she followed them more slowly.

Lynn's glasses were sliding down her nose as she made notations on the roster on her memo board; she gave Jade a weary smile.

"How'd your day go?" Lynn asked.

"A disaster. It's a long, long story," Jade said briefly, staring across at the fence where Lynn's husband, Toby, the head coach, was scratching his head and trying to separate his team from the others. She smiled as she watched and asked Lynn, "The question is, how are you two managing?"

Lynn tossed back her neat ponytail and laughed. "You won't believe this, but we're on top of the world. We're going to have some incredible assistance this year."

"Really? Who? How? Why?"

Toby and Lynn were two of Jade's favorite people in the world. They both worked, shared in the raising of two sons and a daughter and still devoted endless time each year to a new Little League team. The major problem with Little League was the lack of parental interest. Too many people treated it like a babysitting service. Although Jade was incapable of hitting a beach ball with a bat, she'd served as a coach half a dozen times simply for lack of any more qualified volunteers.

"We've got an old pro on our team!" Lynn answered excitedly.

Jade grinned with amusement. "Who do we have? Joe DiMaggio?"

Lynn shook her head. "DiMaggio. Is that the only name you know in baseball?"

"Probably." Jade grinned.

"Well, there's our hero over by the pitching mound."

She pointed down the field. There was a group of parents clustered beneath an oak by the home team bench. They all seemed to be pointing, too, toward the center of the diamond.

Jade shielded her eyes from the sun with the flat of her hand. There was a tall man in shorts and an old football jersey there, showing a child how to pitch. Jade realized first that the child was Sean, and that he was gazing at the newcomer with something akin to awe. All that Jade could tell about the newcomer was that he had longish dark hair beneath the baseball cap he wore.

Jade smiled ruefully, shaking her head. "Who is it?"

Lynn didn't get a chance to answer. Henry Babcock, one of the other parents, tapped her on the shoulder.

"Jade! I just saw your car. What happened?"

"Some jerk hit me this morning," Jade told Henry.

"The driving is getting worse and worse in this city, isn't it?" Henry said. He was still in a suit. Henry was a lawyer with a practice so well established that he could always wrangle the time for baseball practice.

"What a day for it," Lynn noted. "Our new coach got into a tangle this morning, too. He said that a little twit made a left right in front of him."

Jade felt a tingle in her spine even as she told herself that it couldn't be. Miami was a huge city with zillions of fender-benders occurring daily.

But she knew that her fear had been realized when the season's hero, the old pro, approached them.

"Oh, Jade, here he is! Jeffrey Martin! Jeffrey, meet Jade McLane. Sean's mom."

He was a little bit sweaty; he still carried the scent of subtle after-shave. He halted about two feet from Jade, and his startling blue eyes settled on her.

"We've met," he said.

Jade felt as if her jaw had locked. He didn't stretch out a hand to her; both fists remained on his hips.

"You have? Where?" Lynn asked.

Jade felt the heat of his gaze, saw the stubborn set of his jaw. They should have jailed him! she thought furiously.

"This morning," he replied lazily, his eyes never leaving Jade. "At a turn signal on Ponce."

"What—oh." Lynn quickly figured out what he was referring to. For several seconds she was as silent as the hostile pair staring at each other. Then she laughed.

"Okay, then. Twit, meet Jerk. Jerk, meet Twit. Now you can shake hands and come out fighting. But be subtle, please. We have a dozen young men here to whom we're trying to teach sportsmanship."

Jade didn't move, but her hand was suddenly in Jeffrey Martin's. Her palm was engulfed briefly, but firmly, by long, powerful fingers that seemed to radiate heat and energy and tension.

He smiled. Slowly. He had held just her hand, but her entire body grew warm at his touch.

"Maybe you'll let Ryan and me take you and Sean to dinner tonight, Jade. I'd still like to buy you that cup of tea."

He turned and started back toward the boys.

Gritting her teeth, Jade called after him. "Thanks, but n—"

"Jade!" Lynn interrupted her, catching her arm. "Don't you dare be nasty to him! Only the luck of the draw put his son Ryan on Toby's team. This is a dream come true for Toby! And the kids! If you care about any of us—"

"Lynn! He creamed my car and walked away scot-free!"

"What's a car when—"

"It's my only transportation!"

"When compared with the hearts of a dozen little boys. Not to mention that of my husband. Hey! He offered you dinner." Lynn grinned. "If he buys you enough dinners it'll pay for the damage to your car."

"He's a macho egotist! You should have seen him this morning! The cop was falling all over him when he saw his name. I still don't know who or what he supposedly is—"

"Jade! He's one of the greatest pitchers who ever lived. Oh!" Lynn groaned. "Don't you ever read the sports pages? No, you don't, do you? Jeffrey Martin is a candidate for the Hall of Fame! He's got a record for perfect innings!"

"Then what is he doing here?"

"He cracked up his knee in a skiing accident. Sometimes you can see the limp. He was offered a very impressive sum to be a sportscaster down here, so he moved down from Chicago. Jade, come on! His being with us is the chance of a lifetime!"

"Umm," Jade murmured dryly, but her eyes hadn't left Jeffrey Martin. Batting practice had begun, and a small boy with dark hair and wide eyes had just missed every ball that had come his way.

"Good try, Ryan! Fine swing. We just have to get it going in the right direction!" Jeffrey Martin said encouragingly.

The little boy tried to smile. Then he hurried away from the plate, and the next child took his place.

Jeffrey Martin's eyes followed his son with tender concern. But then he had to pitch to the next batter.

Jade found herself watching the little boy. Jeffrey Martin's son. The child was very slim and fragile for such a tall and muscled father. Ryan moved behind the fence, clenching his fingers around it as he watched the other boys. Sean was up next. With his customary finesse, he slammed the ball so hard that it sailed clear out of the field.

Jade cheered for her son with the others, yet her mind wasn't really on him. To her surprise, she discovered that she was walking toward the forlorn-looking child who stood behind the fence.

He was small, so she stooped down when she reached his side.

"Hi. You're Ryan?"

He gazed at her and nodded slowly. She saw that there were tears in his eyes.

Jade smiled. "I'm Sean's mom."

His eyes widened a bit. "Sean's great," he said. He stared at the field again. Kids and grown-ups were still chasing the ball that Sean had hit.

"Sean should have been my dad's kid," he said quietly, then heaved a little sigh.

Well, the father might be a jerk, but the son had captured her heart in those few seconds. If there was anything at all that she wanted to accomplish that season, Jade decided, it was to convince this beautiful little boy that the world was made of much more than macho sports figures.

She forced a little laugh. "Oh, kids and parents don't necessarily do the same things well, Ryan. For example, I like to decorate, but Sean couldn't care less about anything artistic. I'll bet there are things your dad can't do that you'll find you're just great at. And—" she hesitated just briefly "—your dad will be proud of whatever it is that you do well."

Beautiful blue eyes stared into hers hopefully. "You think so?"

"I know so."

Ryan smiled. Jade felt a tingle in her spine, as if she were being watched. She glanced up slowly.

Ryan might not have inherited his father's sports skills, but there was no doubt where he'd gotten the deep and fascinating blue of his eyes.

Jeffrey Martin was staring down at her with a strange look on his face. The lazy smile was gone, and there was something enigmatic and a little dangerous about the intensity of his expression.

The warning tingle shot down her spine again. His apparent nonchalance, she realized, the smile, the laughter, the indolence, was just a facade. There were many layers to this man. There was a ferocity about him, a mysteriousness. Only one thing seemed perfectly clear to her right then: he was a man who would ruthlessly pursue what he wanted.

What was it, she wondered uneasily, that he wanted from her?

Chapter 2

Why in hell had he issued that dinner invitation? Jeff wondered. The woman was nothing short of a bitch.

Didn't matter, he told himself, she'd probably refuse to go, anyway.

"Okay, guys!" he called. "Diamond positions! Let's see if you can snag a few fly balls!"

He idly began to bat balls into the air. The first three bounced on the ground as several boys collided in their efforts to field them. Behind Jeff, Toby began to laugh. Jeff turned around and grinned. Jeff had liked Toby and Lynn the moment he'd met them. Toby was tall and lean and lanky with a gaunt face, slightly crooked teeth and a smile for every kid in town. Lynn was tiny, curvaceous, soft-spoken, but determined. Jeff hadn't intended to coach Little League at all until he'd met Toby, who had enthusiastically urged him to help out.

"It's always like this at the beginning of the season," Toby said, still grinning. "But you watch—they'll come together."

Jeff shrugged and tossed another ball in the air. "This is already more fun than I ever had in the major leagues," he assured Toby as they both watched the ball arc through the air.

This time, the ball was caught. Sean McLane held up his hand, and the ball seemed to slide right into his glove.

"The kid is a natural," Jeff said. He waved as Sean smiled a little shyly, a little proudly.

"Yeah, he is," Toby agree. "And it's ironic."

"Oh? Why?"

"Sean's dad was killed by a baseball bat."

Jeff started. "Murdered?"

"No, no, nothing like that." Toby stepped forward to catch the ball Sean had thrown back. He tossed it into the air for Jeff, continuing to talk as Jeff whacked the ball.

"It was a freak accident. Danny was a deejay. A couple of the stations were having a charity game. All of the guys were fooling around, Danny included. He walked in front of the batter and was hit right at his nape. He was dead in less than five minutes."

Jeff stopped tossing balls. "God, how awful. Was Sean there?"

"Yeah, Sean and Jade."

"Hey! Coach!" one of the kids called.

Jeff mechanically threw another ball into the air. He couldn't stop thinking about Sean and Jade seeing the incident.

"Sean still likes to play? And his mother lets him?"

Toby grinned ruefully. "You can't really stop a kid from playing, can you? Besides, Jade is fairly logical about it. She knows that what happened was a tragic fluke. She has an aversion to sports, but she's been wonderful about helping out with Little League." He shrugged again. "Maybe it's the single-parent syndrome. She divides all her time between work and Sean."

"What does she do?"

"She's a real estate agent." Toby paused as if he'd just thought of something brilliant. "Hey, if you're looking for a house, she'd be perfect."

Perfect? Jeff didn't know about that. He had one strike against him because of the accident. Two strikes, because he was a sports figure.

Three strikes and you're out, my friend....

Out of what, he wondered with annoyance. He batted another ball, then found himself turning to watch her. She was pouring water from a cooler for one of the little boys—he didn't know all their names yet. She smiled, tousled his hair and laughed at something that he said.

He'd asked her out for coffee without ever planning the words. How had he known that she wasn't married? He smiled sardonically. Because she would have been threatening him with her husband if she'd had one.

And then he'd issued that dinner invitation. Why?

Because she was an attractive woman. But there was more to it than that. She hadn't Diana's startling perfection of face and figure, but she had something different and perhaps even more exciting. She made him think of the outdoors, of the country. Her hair had the color of a cornfield beneath the sun; her eyes were a green as deep and endless as the velvet of rolling hills. She was of medium height, and a little thin. But not without padding, he reminded himself, and his grin widened as he realized that he was mentally stripping her, attempting to guess just how she would look nude.

"Hey! Mr. Martin!"

Jeff blinked and looked down. Sean McLane was standing in front of him with a ball.

"Sir, you missed it."

Jeff's mouth twitched with rueful self-reproach. Yes, son. I missed it, because I was thinking about unbuttoning your mother's blouse.

"Thanks, Sean. And hey, you all call Toby by his first name. I'm Jeff, okay?"

Sean gave him a shy smile. It was a good smile, charming and disarming, with full, well-defined lips.

Your mom's smile, Sean, Jeff noted silently. It was her naturalness that attracted him, he decided. The rather wild waves of her thick tawny hair, her eyes, her smile. She was unpolished, but she didn't need make-up or adornment. She moved with a certain sensuality, laughed with pure pleasure and made him think, quite frankly, of wild, spontaneous sex in a jungle setting, or on a beach with waves crashing nearby and the sun overhead.

Hell, he would settle for a bed, a hotel, a motel, the back seat of a car...

Oh, boy. Sorry, Sean, he apologized mentally.

"You're good, son. Really good. Did you know that?"

Sean looked down and shuffled his feet in the red dirt of the diamond. "I, uh, like to play," he said modestly, and Jeff smiled. Then Sean looked up at him. "Do you think I could ever make the Major Leagues?"

"Well—" Out of the corner of his eye, Jeff saw Jade McLane again. All the boys were lined up by the cooler, and she was pouring water. What would her life be, he wondered, if she had to watch her son, week after week, on a baseball diamond?"

She was already doing that, he reminded himself, and apparently doing it well.

"It's a long way off, Sean," Jeff said. "You've got years to see what you really want."

Sean nodded. Jeff felt a tug at the hem of his jersey. He turned to see his son looking at him a little wearily. "Dad? Toby just said we'd call it quits for the day. Do you think we could go eat? I'm starving."

"Yeah, sure. Sean—"

"Hey, Jeff." Toby came up to him and clapped him on the back. "Lynn and I were thinking of taking Barry to the drugstore for supper. Want to come?"

Barry was their nine-year-old son. He was a darned good little player. Not as good as Sean, but few kids had his magic touch.

"I, uh, yeah, I guess. I'd asked Jade if she and Sean would like to join Ryan and me—"

"Good, good, we'll all go together. Hey, listen, stick with us. We'll show you all the real gourmet places."

The drugstore had a fountain and a counter and freshly scrubbed tables and pretty windows. Chicken and meat loaf and various other down-home dishes were served with salads and vegetables and cornbread. The prices were very low, and the waitresses were as pleasant as they could be.

The three boys sat at one table, and the grown-ups seated themselves right next to them. At the kids' table, conversation switched from ball games to the latest in computer games.

Jade McLane, Jeff assumed, had found herself caught between a rock and a hard place. She may have managed to refuse dinner with him, but not with Toby and Lynn. Nor would it have been tactful for her to slide into the seat beside Toby when his wife was present.

She'd had little choice but to sit beside Jeff, and since the tables were small, they were touching. Each time one of them shifted on the seat their thighs brushed together; the slightest movement of a hand or elbow brought their arms in contact.

He wondered if she was as acutely aware of him as he was of her.

She was.

She really couldn't help it, Jade told herself defensively. He was wearing shorts, and they were so damned close that the hair on his calves tickled her flesh right through her stockings.

Thank God it wasn't really necessary for her to participate in the conversation. Toby was busy plotting the upcoming season with Jeff. To Lynn's dismay, he was so engrossed in his plans that he created a diamond with his napkin and four peas.

"Toby!," she exclaimed. "The boys will see you. You just yelled at them for blowing the paper off their straws, and now you're sitting there playing with your peas, for heaven's sake!"

Toby gave Jeff and Jade a long-suffering look, then turned to his wife. "Lynn, I'm not playing with the peas. I'm using them for a purpose. Now—" He turned his attention back to the napkin diamond. "We'll put Chris Garcia on first when Sean is pitching, and vice versa. It will be D. J. or Tommy for second—we'll have to see. And Ryan—"

"Ryan will be outfield," Jeff said. He gave Toby a crooked smile. "He knows he needs a lot of work on his catching."

On catching, on batting, on the whole game, Jade thought. Did Jeff Martin know that his son didn't even like baseball? she wondered. How ironic it was. She, who had to steel her nerves every time the season started, had Sean for a son. And Jeff Martin, a star athlete, had a child who would have been ten times happier in a music or art class than on the ball field. She started to accuse Jeffrey Martin of gross insensitivity, but even as the thought formed, she had to retract it. She had seen the way he looked at his son; she had heard his words of assurance and encouragement. In fact, she couldn't fault Jeff for a single move he had made during the practice. He seemed to be an awful lot like Toby, trying to teach the boys that they should strive to do their best, but letting them know that they were out to have a good time, too.

Toby always applauded Sean, but no more than he did the weakest player on the team for the slightest improvement.

Jeff used the same approach today. When one of the boys missed a ball, he called out, "Almost!" He had promised Mark Craft, who hadn't hit a ball in the three years Sean had been with the league, that his swing was a darned good one, and that once he did hit the ball, it would sail into space.

Jade turned her eyes to the man at her left. Their shoulders were touching, because she had leaned over to catch one of Lynn's comments and Jeff was reaching out to reposition one of Toby's peas.

His eyes were a light blue, like the summer sky, filled with good humor. His dark hair was tousled boyishly over his forehead. He was grinning, and she thought that it was a nice grin. It was very masculine, like the after-shave that clung to him, like the feel of his body, warm and strong against her. He was strikingly good-looking, but his appeal owed as much to his humor and easy manner as to his appearance.

He was the type of man who made you wonder about him just because he looked at you. It was as if there were something hidden inside him, something she longed to explore.

Jade closed her eyes for a minute, feeling a little dizzy. Then why are you so down on him? a voice within her mind demanded. She answered that question easily.

He ran into me! And after he ran into me, he made a fool of me. He conned that stupid cop into letting him off the hook just because he used to throw baseballs around on television.

But what if...what if she hadn't met him until she'd gotten to the Little League practice?

She knew the answer to that one, too. No matter what the circumstances of their meeting, she would have found him frightening and dangerous—on a purely sexual level.

He reminded her of a cunning but lazy wolf, lying in wait, negligently assessing any prey that came too near, then deciding instantly whether to attack.

"Mom?"

"What?" She and Lynn answered the summons simultaneously, laughing when they realized that neither knew which boy had spoken.

"Can we have ice cream?" Barry, it appeared, was the spokesman.

Lynn and Jade shrugged. "Sure," Toby answered. Then his attention went back to Jeffrey. "I can just feel it. We're bound to take the first-place trophy this year."

"Don't count your chickens too soon," Jeffrey said with a laugh as he lifted a hand to the waitress. He asked the boys what kind of ice cream they wanted, then ordered three coffees and a hot tea.

His eyes went to Jade questioningly. "Is it lemon or cream for your tea?"

"Lemon, please," she muttered, and her gaze fell from his.

As the waitress noted her choice Jeff asked for the check. A moment later, Ryan walked around to their table, whispered in his ear, and Jeff nodded, then excused himself to take Ryan to the bathroom.

"I don't want him picking up the check," Jade said in a hushed tone when the two were gone.

Lynn was putting cream into her coffee. "Oh, come on, Jade, don't be silly."

"I—"

"Jade, you'd let me pick up the check," Toby told her dryly. "Hell, I'd even let you pick up the check here. It's cheap."

Jade made a face at him. "Damn you, Toby, I'm not a poverty case!"

"If the real estate market slows down any more, you will be," Lynn said matter-of-factly. "What is the problem here, anyway?"

Jade felt cornered, a little defensive and ridiculously confused. "I'm going to pay this check!" she said, raising a hand to summon the waitress. She leaned closer to Lynn and muttered, "I don't want that reckless jackass—"

She broke off because Lynn looked as if she had swallowed her napkin and Toby had turned a startling shade of crimson. An uneasy feeling crawled along her spine, and she turned. Of course, her "jackass" was standing right next to the table, watching her politely. He slid beside her again and smiled.

"What did I miss?" he asked softly.

Weren't the real pro baseball players supposed to chew tobacco, spit—and break anything that got in their way?

She wasn't sure, nor was she sure why she backed down. Maybe she realized that she was being unreasonable. Maybe it was because she believed that Toby was about to deck her if Jeffrey Martin didn't.

She smiled a little sickly, but it was a smile. "Nothing!" she said brightly.

"Yes, may I help you?"

Jade glanced around to see that the waitress had come. She realized that her hand was still in the air.

"I'd, uh, could I get another cup of tea, please?"

The waitress went to get her another cup of tea. Toby's color returned to normal, and it seemed that Lynn was breathing again.

"You still have tea in your cup, Mrs. McLane," Jeffrey Martin commented in a low tone.

She looked at him sharply, realized that he was laughing at her and wished she had the nerve to empty the tea in his lap.

"So I do," she demured sweetly. She drank it in one swallow, feeling like an idiot.

Oh, God. Her entire day had been a disaster from start to finish, and all thanks to Jeffrey Martin.

She began to pray that the check would come, and at last it did. She gulped down her unwanted second cup of tea and managed a stiff thank-you for dinner.

And then, thank God, they were all leaving the restaurant, going to their separate cars. She would have peace at last.

Unfortunately, there was to be no peace, not really. All the way home, Sean talked about Jeffrey Martin. Jade's fingers curled tightly around the steering wheel, and she managed to refrain from screaming at him to please shut up. It was particularly difficult when he said, "Wow! I can't believe it was Jeffrey Martin you crashed into!"

"He crashed into me!"

Sean didn't answer her. She wanted to throttle her own son.

It didn't take her long to head back down Sunset and wind onto Main Highway, then turn left down the road that would take her to her driveway. There was little traffic that night. Driving through the dense foliage that lined her driveway and made it seem longer, she felt a sense of immense relief. She was home, safe in her haven behind the banyans and the seagrapes and the crotons. She would take a hot shower, lie down, remind Sean to do his homework and try to pretend that the day had never occurred.

Jade parked the car and reached into the back of the Corvette for Sean's school books. "Get into the shower quickly," she began. "It's already late—"

She stopped, frowning, as a pair of headlights followed her into the yard. Then she swore softly and ground her teeth.

It was Jeffrey Martin.

The lights on his car flicked off. A second later he and Ryan got out of the car, and Sean—what a traitor—raced over to them. "Hi!"

"Hi, Scan. I just needed to speak with your mother for a minute."

"Oh, good! Well, can you come in for a bit? I can show Ryan the team picture from last year."

Come in? Sean, I could... Jade didn't allow herself to finish the thought. She had been standing in the walkway with Sean's books, and now she was obliged to open the door.

"Can we, Dad?" Ryan asked hopefully.

Jade shoved Sean's books unceremoniously into his arms and smiled at Ryan. He was a sweetheart—quite unlike his father. He must have more in common with his mother, she thought.

Mother. Where was Ryan's mother, anyway. Jade wondered. His father was definitely unencumbered by a wife.

"Of course, Ryan," she said, quickly finding the right keys for the front door and opening it. Despite her annoyance at the intrusion, she quickly scanned the living room as she turned on the light; she was hoping that it was all tidy.

It was. Pretty much so, anyway. There was a pile of clean laundry on the sofa, but as the others followed her in, she swept it up into her arms and quickly dumped it on the washer in the kitchen before returning to the living room.

"C'mon, Ryan, I'll show you my room!" Sean said, and the two boys loped off together like a pair of gangly greyhounds.

Jade waited until they had disappeared down the hallway. Then she smoothed back a strand of hair and stared coldly at Jeffrey Martin.

"What do you want?"

He laughed and moved into the room, assessing it as thoroughly and quickly as he had her.

He approached her, arms crossed over his chest, blue eyes alive with amusement. "Not your virtue, person or property," he assured her in a way that caused her to blush.

"What, then?"

"Toby told me that you're a real estate agent."

Her eyes flickered downward for a moment. This wasn't what she had expected at all.

"Yes. Why?"

"I need a house."

"Oh." Jade took a breath, thought about the damaged Corvette, and thought about his rugged, unnerving appeal.

"Mr. Martin, I really don't think that we could work well together."

"Oh?" He didn't seem distressed. He paused in front of the piano and picked up one of the sleek Art Deco ashtrays sitting there. He traced the form with his thumb, a motion that somehow disturbed her. Maybe it was because the handle of the ashtray was a sculptured woman, and his thumb was idly moving over her breast.

He set the ashtray down and turned back to her.

"Why is that?"

"Why? Because of this morning!"

"Oh, that," he said dismissively.

"Oh, that? You ruined my car!"

He sighed. "Mrs. McLane, I'll fix your damned car."

"No!"

He shook his head, still smiling in that amused manner that so irritated her. "Mrs. McLane, I really can't quite get this. You're running around raving that I'm a jackass because of your car; I offer to fix the car, and you're still raving."

"I don't want your charity, Mr. Martin. I wanted you to get the ticket that you deserved. Then your insurance company could have paid for the car."

"Are you afraid of me for some reason?"

"Don't be ridiculous."

"Then?"

"Then, what?"

He grimaced, walked around the room once and settled himself comfortably in the Duncan Fife sofa she had saved from a secondhand shop and painstakingly refurbished herself.

"Nice house," he commented, looking around at the old Spanish-style arches. "Something like what

I'm looking for. I'd want something a little larger, though."

"Don't be so sure that you want one of these," Jade answered mechanically. "Twenties architecture might be young in the north, but it's very old down here, and these things eat money. They need new insulation, the roofs almost always need repair and—"

She stopped. How had she wound up talking to him about houses?

"Go on," he told her, and she realized that he really was interested. He was leaning forward, hands folded between his knees, his eyes on her intently.

She sighed. "They're a big expense, but once restored, they usually have a high resale value. There's very little new building in the Grove or in the Gables. Not in this section. There is, of course, a great deal of new construction going on in Greater Miami. It all depends on where you want to live."

He smiled. "Somewhere around here. Gables or Grove. On a waterway, if possible. Open to the bay."

Jade bit her lip. Waterway property was expensive. The commission from the sale of a waterway property would be very nice.

She hesitated, watching him. She found herself wondering again what her feelings would be if it hadn't been for their smashup that morning. Wouldn't she have jumped at a chance like this? Suppose he was...a little intimidating, even dangerous. Sexually, that is. She was an adult. She knew how to say no.

She had to face the fact that there really wasn't any way to avoid him completely. She could hardly pull Sean off Toby's team.

"What, ah, price range are you looking for?" she asked him.

He lifted his hands. "I really have no idea. I want to be on the water, and I want at least four bedrooms and three baths. Oh, and a pool." Something seemed to cloud his eyes. "I've moved Ryan down to the sun and heat; maybe he'll like swimming." He looked at her again, his eyes clearing, his negligent smile back in place. "I'd like to see things in a range of prices first, and try to find out what property values are like down here."

Her mouth didn't seem to work properly.

"When?"

"When?"

She forced the words out. "When would you like to start looking?"

"I'm off Friday mornings."

"Ten o'clock?"

"Fine."

He stood up then, his business finished. "Ryan!"

Ryan either didn't hear the call, or he did hear it and preferred to ignore it.

Jeffrey looked at Jade again. His gaze was curious, as if he still had questions about her, but had already discovered certain answers. She wished she knew what the questions were, and what conclusions he had reached.

"They've probably started playing something," she muttered, walking past him. "I'll get them."

She crossed the living room to the hallway that led to the bedrooms. The hall light was on, as was the light in Sean's room. She quickly walked to his door. As she had suspected, the boys were playing. Ryan was laughing delightedly as Sean showed him some of his toys.

"Ryan, your dad wants to leave," Jade said.

He looked up at her with his huge blue eyes, and she had the urge to go to him and hug him. She wanted to assure him that everything would be all right, though what could be wrong, she didn't know. It was obvious that his father adored him, and certainly there were no financial difficulties in Ryan's life.

"Already?" Sean demanded defensively.

"Yes, already," Jade retorted.

"Come along now, Ryan."

Jade jumped at the male voice behind her; she hadn't heard Jeffrey follow her. Now she realized that he was so close that his breath was fanning her hair and her neck. She quivered at the warm, disturbing sensation.

She couldn't turn around. She remained fixed to the spot as Ryan thanked Sean, and Sean replied, "Anytime!" It wasn't until Ryan came to her, thanked her very politely and walked past her, that she turned.

"I'll see you Friday," Jeffrey told her over Ryan's head.

"No! Thursday. Another practice!" Sean reminded him.

"That's right." Jeff grinned at Sean. "How could I forget?"

He started down the hall, a hand on Ryan's shoulder. Jade followed the pair; Sean rushed past her to tug at Jeffrey Martin's jersey tail.

"You wouldn't really forget, would you?" Sean asked him earnestly. "I mean, you are going to be around for the whole season?"

Jeffrey touched his hair. "I wouldn't really forget, Sean. And yes, you're stuck with me—for the whole season."

And then he was out the door, pausing only to look around the porch and into the darkened yard.

"Oh, yes," he told her. "One more thing. I want foliage like this. Do you know what I mean? I like this much better than all those overly manicured yards."

"I'll start looking through the listings tomorrow," she told him, then hesitated. "I can, uh, copy some listing sheets and bring them to practice."

"Thanks. Thanks a lot," he replied. Then he was gone.

Jade stared after him, her eyes on the closed door for too long a time. She gave herself a mental shake and bolted the locks.

Then she turned around to find Sean staring at her. "Hey!" she said. "Now it's later than ever. Get going. Into the shower. Then homework."

"Sure." Sean grinned and went down the hall whistling.

Within another hour, Sean had bathed and finished his homework and was in bed. He was allowed to watch television until nine-thirty, as long as he did so in bed.

At last Jade was free to run hot water into her own tub. She added a liberal amount of bath oil, pulled her hair on top of her head and leaned back. Then she tried to assess her reactions to Jeffrey Martin.

If her anger over the car were gone...

She shook her lead slightly. If it were gone, she would still be hesitating. She couldn't help it; his kind of masculinity scared her. She didn't form relationships easily, and she had never been "casually" involved with anyone. She'd only fallen in love once—with Danny. And that love had been painful.

Painful . . . and then tragic.

Jeffrey Martin was magnetic. He could look at a woman and make her feel like the most sensual creature on earth. He made a woman want to purr and curl up on his lap.

She was sure that a number of women had done just that. Purely physical relationships were perfectly all right, she told herself. A lot of her friends preferred to have light flings instead of getting involved.

"But I couldn't be like that," she said aloud.

Then she understood what she was afraid of. He wanted her. At least she was fairly certain that he did. But after he'd had her, what then? Would he give her a kiss goodbye and move on to the next woman?

She sighed, exhaling long and miserably. She barely knew him. Maybe in the days to come she would discover that she really didn't like him.

She doubted it.

"Be wary, Mrs. McLane," she warned herself out loud.

Be wary, be careful, keep your distance. . . .

But that wouldn't be so easy. He had made her think of things that she hadn't dared dwell on in a long time now. It seemed like forever since she'd been with a man who could make her laugh, excite her with just the sound of his voice, thrill her . . . cause hurt again.

She got out of the bathtub, telling herself that she was crazy. Men like Jeffrey Martin probably didn't get involved. Not with ordinary women like her, at any rate. And if she let herself think any differently, she was a fool who deserved whatever she got.

"What am I thinking of," she asked herself irritably. "He's still the jerk who wrecked my car!"

But long past midnight, she was still awake. At 1:00 a.m., she gave up, went into the kitchen and consumed two glasses of wine.

The wine didn't really help. It made her wonder what it would be like to have a casual fling just once in her life.

Chapter 3

On Wednesday, Jade spent several hours looking through the multiple listings for Gables/Grove properties on the water. She researched everything she found, certain that for all Jeffrey Martin's casual ease, he would barrage her with sharp and intelligent questions on everything she showed him.

She hesitated occasionally. Some of the listings were priced over the half a million mark. Then she shrugged and decided he'd just have to find out how expensive it was to be finicky in South Florida.

Her fingers tightened around her pencil. Generally, the realtor's commission was six percent of the sale. If her customer bought another agent's property, the split was fifty-fifty. One of the benefits of working in a small office was that she kept three-quarters of that three percent; the firm took only one-quarter. In the big companies, the realtor only received half of three percent.

Jade didn't think that she was a mercenary person. She was a good realtor and always tried to show her clients homes within their financial limits. She was careful to point out the negative aspects of a property as well as the positive. She knew the school system, the flood zones and the heavy taxation areas. From experience, she knew that the beautiful old Spanish houses could also be monsters, always demanding repair. She steered people with limited incomes into more modest neighborhoods.

But she couldn't help hoping that Jeffrey Martin would buy a very expensive house.

"And if it proves to be too much, you can choke on it!" she cursed aloud.

"Who can choke on what?"

Sandy had stuck his head curiously out of his office doorway. Jade flushed, then told him about the previous evening, and how the man who had crashed into her had now become a client.

Sandy, to her annoyance, was impressed with the name Jeffrey Martin. "I'm going to have to go to one of those practices and get his autograph. Genevieve, this is your lucky month." Sandy was one of the few people who ever used her real name. He shook his head happily. "Imagine that! First you get Mr. Harrison's property. Then you crash into a baseball great, and he becomes your customer, anyway."

"He crashed into me!"

The protestation made no difference. Sandy was gone, Jade decided that all men were jerks. Mention sports and they all turned into awe-struck little kids.

It didn't occur to her until Sean was in bed for the night that she really didn't have to go to practice on Thursday afternoon. Timmy Hodges's mother was supposed to pick the boys up and take them to practice. All that Jade had to do was swing by and find Sean when it was all over.

She glanced at the listings she had been studying and caught her lower lip between her teeth. She really needed to sell Jeffrey something. Quickly. The market had been depressed for a long time and her last sale had been a small house down in Perrine.

She hesitated only a second longer, picked up the phone and called Miriam Hodges, telling her that she'd go to school to pick up Timmy and Sean. Miriam was glad—she was very involved in her tennis lessons and could put in another hour or so working on her backhand.

Jade replaced the receiver with a wry smile. More power to you, Miriam.

"I wonder if I'll ever have the time and money to take tennis lessons," she mused aloud and then laughed because she didn't even know if she would like to play tennis.

Her laughter faded and her smile became bittersweet. If Danny were alive, she would have fewer financial worries. They wouldn't have remained married; she knew that. Danny had needed more variety and excitement out of life than she could provide. But he would have taken care of her, and she would have loved him always.

One of his best qualities had been his adoration of his son. She and Danny might have divorced, but he never would have shirked his parental responsibility.

He would have seen to it that the roof was fixed. He would have made sure that the Corvette was repaired.

Jade slipped her papers into a folder with the name Jeffrey Martin neatly penned across it. Then she rose quickly to press her clothes for the following morning. She didn't want to sit there thinking about Danny. His death always brought tears to her eyes, but there was nothing she could do to change the past.

On Thursday Jade found she was alarmingly nervous. The events of the afternoon, however, were a letdown. She didn't know what she had expected, but Jeffrey Martin barely spoke to her. He accepted the folder with a simple "Thanks," set it aside and gave his attention to batting practice.

Lynn was the only other mother present that day. All the fathers had found ways to slip out of work to bring their kids to the park. Word had gotten out that Jeffrey Martin was the new assistant coach, and the guys had come out en masse to meet him.

At the end of practice, he handed the folder back to Jade. "I marked off the ones I don't want to see," he told her. "The rest look interesting."

He didn't suggest dinner. She was surprised to realize that she would have gone without a thought.

Sean was talkative all the way home. "Toby says I have to pitch the second half of the game all the time. That's so that if we fall behind, we can try to catch up. If we're behind at the beginning, and can't pitch the other guys out in the second half, we won't have a prayer." He fell silent for a minute. "You know, it's funny that Ryan can't pitch worth beans. You would think he'd be great. I mean, he lives with his dad. He's got Jeff to help him all the time. Boy, if Jeff were my dad, I could be really great.''

Sean sounded envious. Jade clenched her teeth together.

"Don't brag," she said. "You know I hate it. And if you do too much of it, you won't have any friends, no matter how well you pitch. I'm sure that Ryan is very good at something else—like math, maybe, which is much more important in the long run.

"Not if I make the Major Leagues."

"Sean, you're nine years old. Drop it." She exhaled and turned on the radio. Then she said, "Sean, you *are* very good, and I'm proud of you. But there are—"

"Lots more things in life. I know."

She turned the radio up. Sean spoke above it, anyway.

"Mom!"

"What?"

His lower lip was trembling a little, and she turned the radio down.

"My father wasn't killed because of the game, you know. What happened to Dad was..."

He was going to start crying. And if he did, she would. She gripped his hand. "I know, Sean. Did you decide what you want to do for your science project yet?"

Sean muttered out a negative reply, then turned the radio back up himself.

Jade told herself that she was being a little bitchy and that he was just being a kid. He had a right to love baseball, and a right to want her approval when he did well. It was that damned Jeffrey Martin again. Tonight, the problem wasn't that he had plagued her, she was annoyed because he had ignored her.

"I'm going to take a quick shower before I start dinner. Just hot dogs tonight, okay?" she asked as they went into the house.

Sean was agreeable. He liked hot dogs.

Jade slipped out of her dusty sandals and clothing, showered and put on a long satin robe. Sean was seated at the kitchen table finishing his homework when she came out. She rummaged in the freezer for the hot dogs and started when the doorbell rang.

"I'll get it!" Sean said.

"Hey!" She called after him. "Make sure you see who it is first!" Nighttime visitors always made her a little nervous. Unfortunately, the Grove was known for crime as well as beauty.

"Hi! Come on in!"

Jade wanted to clobber Sean. Here she was in a robe, wearing no makeup, with damp hair plastered to her face and he was inviting people in.

She hurried to the kitchen doorway and winced.

Jeffrey Martin and Ryan were there. Ryan was still in his dusty baseball pants; Jeffrey was still in his jogging shorts and gray T-shirt.

His eyes met hers across the room and the curl of an elusive smile touched one corner of his lips. She wanted to shrink back into the kitchen, and then she wanted to kick herself for caring how he saw her.

"I'm sorry. We didn't mean to disturb you. Your phone number isn't listed, and we didn't make arrangements for a place to meet in the morning."

"Oh." She was annoyed at her stupidity. "The, uh, office is north of where we're looking. I thought we'd start off in Cocoplum; I have keys to all those houses. Our first actual appointment is at eleven—"

"Shall I just pick you up here?"

Again she hesitated. "I should probably drive. I know the area better than you."

He shook his head. "I'll drive. I'll be here at . . . what . . . nine-thirty?"

"Uh, yeah, I suppose that will be fine."

"Hot dogs!" Ryan said suddenly. Jade realized that she was holding the pack in her hands, and that Ryan was looking as enviously at her as Sean had spoken about Jeff earlier.

She had to smile. His eyes were so big, so hopeful.

Why didn't Jeffrey Martin have a bratty little kid she could dislike?

The words were out of her mouth before she realized that she had spoken them. "You haven't had dinner yet, Ryan?"

"No, ma'am."

"Ryan!" Jeffrey spoke sharply. "We're not—"

Jade found herself rushing to Ryan's defense. "It's fine, really. If you don't mind just hot dogs, chips and salad, you're very welcome to stay for dinner."

Jeffrey's jaw had hardened, but for once, Jade had pleased her own son. He was giving her a big smile of approval. "Please, coach?" he asked Jeff. He didn't wait for an answer, but told Ryan, "We can take out the stuff I was showing you the other night—"

"You cannot, young man. You can finish your homework."

"But I need help with the centimeters—"

"I can help you, Sean," Ryan said. "Really, I can help him, Mrs. McLane."

"Call her Jade. All the other kids do."

Ryan looked at his father anxiously. "Can we stay, Dad? Can we, please?"

He threw up his hands in defeat, but he still didn't appear particularly pleased. Jade gave him a wry smile.

"Hey," she reminded him softly, "we did wind up being your dinner guests last Tuesday."

"We didn't come for dinner."

Jade smiled again and returned to the kitchen. Sean followed her, snatching up his books and promising that Ryan would help him in his bedroom. Jade took out another pack of hot dogs.

She was running them beneath hot water to defrost them before putting them beneath the broiler when she realized that she wasn't alone. Jeffrey had followed her in. He was sitting on top of the dryer, legs dangling. "Can I help?"

She shook her head. "Not really. I was dead serious. It's just hot dogs."

There was an awkward silence. Jade wished she wasn't standing there like a half-drowned rat. She wondered why it was that his being in the room made it a different place. Why she felt as if something inside her had caught fire.

She dug the lettuce and tomatoes out of the refrigerator and then exclaimed, "Oh! Would you like a drink? I don't have much of a choice. I think there's some Scotch. And beer. No—I don't have any beer, I'm sorry. Toby was over here about a week ago and he finished off the last of the six-pack. I have some wine. White and red. I wonder which is supposed to be proper for hot dogs."

He laughed and slid off his perch on the dryer. "I always say it's proper to drink white with anything—if you prefer white wine. And equally proper to drink red with anything—if you prefer red."

He was standing next to the refrigerator, grinning. Slowly, she returned his smile, but she moved back along the counter to put some distance between them.

"I think I like that rule," she said. "Mind helping yourself? The white is in the refrigerator; the red is at the end of the counter."

He reached for the red, Jade noticed.

"Glasses?"

"Right above you."

He poured a glass of red wine. "And for you?"

"White, please."

He poured a glass for her. He didn't hand it to her, but set it on the counter before her. Jade was alarmed at the disappointment that their hands hadn't touched. It was crazy to want that kind of contact with him.

He reached into the pocket of his shorts. She heard his keys jingle, then he pulled out a pack of cigarettes.

"Mind if I smoke?"

"No. There's an ashtray at the end of the counter, too."

He lit a cigarette, found the ashtray and leaned against the counter, watching her. Jade tried to give her attention to the lettuce. Even though she refused to look at him, she was all too aware of his presence. He hadn't seemed quite so... naked out on the diamond. Now she kept recalling the way his cutoff T-shirt ended at his ribs, that the three inches of bare stomach beneath it were bronzed and tight and just slightly rippled with muscle. His shorts didn't leave much to the imagination, either. His thighs were muscled and dark from the sun. His long legs were those of a runner.

"I didn't realize that you smoke," Jade mumbled, searching for something to say, something to break the silence. She took a long sip of her wine.

He leaned an elbow on the counter. His eyes touched her lightly; they were filled with amusement, as usual.

"I don't often," he said simply. "Only when I'm nervous."

A surge of adrenaline went through her. She swallowed too much wine and bent over the stove to hide her coughing.

"Why on earth would you be nervous?" she asked, turning the hots dogs.

"I don't really know."

He inhaled very slowly on his cigarette. Jade realized with dawning horror that his gaze was fixed on the satin V of her robe. Her bent position had caused the neckline to dip, and from his vantage point she probably appeared naked to the waist.

Embarrassment warmed her much more than the heat of the oven. She pulled her robe together and slammed the oven shut. Oh! What if he thought she had purposely chosen that position? Oh, God. This was worse than looking like a drowned rat. She imagined she could feel his gaze. It was as if he could actually touch her with his eyes, feather her breasts with a gentle stroke....

"It's...strange. That anything at all could make you nervous," she said finally, and she added silently, You're the most nerve-racking man I've ever met!

"Oh, we're all human, you know." My God, he was thinking, you've got the most beautiful breasts I've ever seen.

She stared at him and smiled a little awkwardly. "The plates. Would you mind?"

She reached for the plates in the cupboard above the sink. He took them from her. His fingers did brush hers then. They felt just like fire. She lowered her eyes. They fell on the bare patch of taut muscled flesh just above his waistband.

"Where do you want them set?" he asked, but his mind was on other things. That slip of nothing she was wearing must be satin. He could see her nipples against it and they were beautiful. "In the kitchen?"

"Yes, we'll eat in here." How could he possibly smell so wonderful? she asked herself privately.

"Want to give me the forks and napkins, too?"

"Oh, yes. Thanks.

Jade wrenched open the silverware drawer and piled utensils on top of the plates. Then she backed away from him, feeling that she was surely beet red. "I, uh, think I'll throw some jeans on," she mumbled. And then she ran.

She tore into her room, dug wildly through her dresser, avoided her reflection in the mirror and ignored the fact that she was totally destroying the order of her drawer in her haste to slip into a bra. She still didn't feel safe from the traitorous effects of her body, so she went through the closet until she found a loose shirt.

She was breathing too quickly; she forced herself to take in deep gulps of air.

All this from a conversation about forks and plates? It was ridiculous.

She bit her lower lip lightly and slipped on a pair of jeans, determined to go back out and behave normally. When she reached the kitchen, she found that was easier than she had expected. In her absence, the boys had made an appearance. Jeff had taken the hot dogs out of the oven, set the salad on the table and seated himself next to Ryan.

And Sean was being, as usual, quite adept at talking up a storm. "Wow! I finished all that math, Mom. Do you believe it? Ryan told me what I was doing wrong, and I finished it! That quickly."

"That's wonderful," Jade said. "Do we need anything else?"

"Grace."

Sean rattled off the prayer so quickly that Jade was amazed he got all the syllables in. And when he was done, he continued to talk nonstop, telling Jeff and Ryan all about the slumber party Toby and Lynn had at the beginning of each season. For once, she was grateful that Sean had the capacity to be a real motor mouth. She was saved from having to add much to the conversation during the meal.

But the boys finished quickly, too quickly. And then she was left alone again with Jeffrey Martin.

Jade played with her salad, trying to find something to look at, anything but him.

"Ryan seems to be a very bright child," she remarked finally.

"Yes. He is. He's lucky. He catches on to things quickly."

"Was...is his mother sharp like that?" What was she doing, she wondered in dismay, trying to find out about his personal life?

Jeff laughed. "Does that mean that I'm supposed to be stupid? That he couldn't possibly have inherited such qualities from me?"

"No!" she said quickly, glancing up at him. In response to the wry amusement in his eyes she went on hurriedly. "I didn't mean that. It's just that, uh, well, sports is obviously what you do well. And—"

"And baseball players are dumb clucks who chew tobacco and scratch their heads if someone asks them what the capital of the state is?"

"I didn't say that at all!"

"You didn't have to."

Jade stood and began clearing the table. She turned her back to him, running water over a plate.

"You didn't answer my question," she reminded him.

"Is Diana particularly brilliant? No, I don't believe she's going to take any Nobel prizes. She's smart, though, when she chooses to be."

With her back to him, Jade was able to wince without his noticing. What was she doing? she berated herself. They could talk about the weather; they could talk about his new job. They could talk about half a million things, and here she was prying into his personal life.

Her motive for doing so was what really disturbed her. She was dying to touch him, to run her fingers through the dark hair that waved across his forehead, to place her palms against his cheeks and test the texture of his skin. She wanted to run her knuckles over the taut muscles between the waistline of his shorts and the edge of his shirt . . .

"What does she do?"

Oh, hell, oh, hell, a thousand times over. She didn't want to fall for a man like this one. He was too handsome, too rugged, too sexual. She needed a professor, a librarian, a skinny accountant, someone with his nose always in a book, his heart in his home.

Jeff was on his feet, clearing dishes behind her and setting them on the counter.

"Whatever she wants, usually," was his brief reply.

Don't look at me right now, she thought. Please don't look at me right now.

"You're divorced, I take it?"

"Of course." He was silent for a moment, and she thought his voice had a bitterness to it when he spoke again. "I see. As a 'dumb, tobacco-chewing, hick baseball player' I would have asked you to dinner the other night whether I was free or not."

"I didn't say that!"

"And again, Mrs. McLane, you didn't have to. Want the ketchup back in the refrigerator?"

Jade spun around. "Stop making me sound so bigoted!"

He opened the refrigerator. "Top shelf?" he asked, his eyes slightly narrowed.

"Yes. Thank you. I'm sorry, Mr. Martin. I'm sure you're quite respectable."

"I think so, yes."

"All you really wanted the other morning was coffee."

"The other morning, yes. What about the mustard? Top shelf, too?"

"Yes!"

Frustrated, she turned around and attacked the dishes again with a vengeance. "Then I do extend my apologies, Mr. Martin. You're most certainly a saint. I have nothing whatever to fear. You're not interested in—"

"Your body? Sleeping with you?" he suggested, leaning against the refrigerator.

She wanted to throw the sponge at him. Heat washed through her again; she felt a tremor of excitement that made her want to scream at herself in fury for being a fool.

"Of course," she said as blithely as she could manage. "You're not after a single thing except a house and a platonic friendship."

He laughed. "Now that, Mrs. McLane, is something that I most assuredly didn't say, either."

He moved away from the refrigerator. "Ryan!" he called. "It's late, we've got to go!"

Ryan appeared almost instantly. Maybe the boy recognized a deadly tone when he heard it. For despite Jeff's amusement, she had angered him, Jade realized. He was cool and distant when he turned back to her.

"Thank you for dinner. I'll see you in the morning. Ryan, tell Mrs. McLane thank-you."

Ryan did that dutifully and Jade wanted to hug him. He had such a fragile look about him. He seemed so eager for approval.

"You're welcome, Ryan. It was very nice having you."

Ryan beamed; Jeff tousled Sean's hair and said good-night. He didn't glance at Jade again. The door closed behind him, and Jade discovered herself locking it very quickly—as if she could lock out the devil.

"I'm going to take care of him, Mom."

"What?" Jade turned around to see Sean standing there with a faraway expression in his eyes. His hands were on his hips, and there was a stubborn cast to his jaw.

"Ryan. Some of the kids were teasing him today 'cause he couldn't pitch anyone out. But I like him. And I'm going to take care of him."

He turned around and started for his bedroom. Jade watched him.

"Hey!" she called.

He paused and turned around to look at her.

"I love you," she told him.

He grinned slowly, then ran back and gave her a big hug. She hugged him back, very glad that there were still times when he was a little boy, little enough to be cuddled and held when she needed very badly to be cuddled and hugged in return.

Chapter 4

Jade knew Jeffrey was outside before he tapped at the door. She'd heard the low hum of his car and had watched him from the window as he parked, got out and walked around her Corvette a number of times. He looked very "Miami" that day, she thought, in off-white slacks, a casual white jacket over a knit shirt and no tie. The outfit was fashionable, and he wore it well. His hair was very dark against the light suit, his features tanned and healthy. She found herself wondering exactly how old he was, what he did to keep up the deep dark tan, the muscles, what he looked like shaving in the morning...

She gave herself a little shake as he came up the porch steps, and hurried to the door to be there when he knocked.

"Hi. You're early," she said.

"Am I?"

"I made coffee. Want some?"

He grinned slowly. "I thought you didn't drink it."

"I don't, but I know how to make it."

"Sure, I'd love some."

A few minutes later, he was seated at the kitchen table with a cup of coffee, and Jade was across from him. As usual, she was acutely aware of him. He had just shaved. She liked the texture of his cheek. His hair was still damp from a shower. Jade couldn't sit still, not while she was so close to him. She jumped up and produced a map of the area, showing him U.S.1, the Grove, Main, Sunset and the uneven splotches of property where the Gables began and ended. She leaned over the map, trying to explain the divisions.

"Greater Miami is really twenty-seven municipalities. South Miami, Miami Beach, Miami Shores, et cetera. Coral Gables is a municipality, Coconut isn't. It's a section of the main city. It makes a difference when it comes to taxes and laws. Coral Gables is strict—you need permits for anything you build. But, the property values always remain high because the neighborhoods are so nice. The Grove is intriguing, and property values in the Grove stay high just because it's the Grove. It's a strange place—you have million-dollar mansions, medium housing and ghettos, one on top of another. In the end, it all comes out to where you decide you want to be."

She had leaned over his shoulder to point out various areas on the map. He turned to her curiously, and she realized their faces were almost touching.

"You didn't get your car fixed yet."

"I haven't had time," she lied quickly, moving away from him. She glanced at her watch. "I guess we'd better get going."

His car, she discovered as she climbed into the passenger's seat, was a Lincoln Town Car. Strange, she mused, that she hadn't really noticed what it was when the damned thing had made mince meat out of her Corvette.

Well, now she knew. A Lincoln Town Car. Nice, she decided a little bitterly. Roomy, and very comfortable. The stereo system was wonderful, the air conditioning quiet, and the seats so comfortable that she thought she could curl up and go to sleep.

"Where to?"

"I thought we'd just drive first."

"Fine. Where?"

She directed him to the road leading past the guard tower into Gables Estates. Waterways came into view, and on either side of the road were immense homes that looked like country clubs.

"Are we going into any houses here?" he asked her.

She shook her head. "No, not today. We can, though." She smiled. "I was going to show you a lot that is for sale. It curves right onto the open water, near the Wackenhut castle.

"It's quite an area," he said admiringly.

A few minutes later they parked and got out to walk around the lot. It had been cleared, but there were a few palms left, their fronds drifting in the cool breeze from the bay.

"What do you think?"

"It's nice. I'd still like something more overgrown, with shrubs and trees and all."

It's nice—that was all he had to say about Gables Estates. She lifted her nose a little. "Just as well. This land alone will go for about eight hundred thousand or more."

He didn't say anything but led the way back to the car. Their next stop was Cocoplum. Jade showed him a number of new homes, exquisite houses, with every modern convenience: beveled glass windows, marble floors, high-tech kitchens, decorator family rooms and designer pools. He barraged her with questions about square footage, construction, wiring, lot size and so on. She answered them all, grateful that she had prepared herself so well.

Their third stop was on a waterway with "no bridges to the bay" in the south Gables. The house had been built in the thirties; it had beautiful turrets and balconies, a spiral staircase and a separate guesthouse. She knew that he liked it far more than he had the others, and she decided that she would be smart to show him older homes from here on out. The owner was home to go through the house with them, so it wasn't until she left them in the yard sloping down to the water that he told her his real thoughts.

"This is more of what I had in mind, except that it's too small."

"It's twenty-five hundred square feet. Three bedrooms, three baths. How many rooms do you need for two people?"

He laughed. "More than this. I'm going to have to hire a live-in housekeeper. And I'm not planning on being 'two' forever."

He was staring out at the water, hands in his pockets. The breeze ruffled his hair.

She felt restless, as if she wanted to get very close to him and run away at the same time. She couldn't begin to hazard a guess at his feelings, but she kept remembering what he'd said when she had suggested that he was interested only in a platonic relationship. "I didn't say that, either," he had told her. Yet today he had been all business. He had opened her car door with perfunctory courtesy at each stop; he hadn't touched her at all. Not even casually.

"You've got a remarriage all planned?" she asked with what she hoped was casual humor.

He kept staring at the water. "Sure," he said with a shrug. "I'd like to marry again. I like commitment, family life."

"You make it sound very easy."

"I still believe that it can be." He looked at her then, his eyes the color of the midday sky. "You sound skeptical, Mrs. McLane. But you're a widow, not a divorcée."

Jade turned around. She wasn't about to tell him that though she had loved Danny with all her heart, her marriage had been on the rocks right from the start.

"Let's go, shall we? We have an appointment in five minutes."

He liked the next house, too. The owners had meticulously restored it to its original grandeur, and it was gracious as well as modern. It was located on the water; it had a dock for a yacht. It had four bedrooms and was almost four thousand square feet.

"The only problem here," he told her with a sigh, "is that the yard is too small."

"It's a half acre!" Jade protested. "Land is at a premium here, you know!"

"But surely you can find me more of it."

"Only if you want to spend a fortune," Jade advised him.

He shrugged. "Is this it for the day?"

"Yes, this is our last appointment."

"Let's go get some lunch."

She opened her mouth to protest, then wondered why she should. She didn't have to be anywhere today until it was time to pick up Sean. Sandy didn't expect her to come into the office. Besides, she rationalized, Jeffrey Martin was a client, one who might bring her badly needed income.

"All right. Where?"

"You pick the place, madame."

She smiled as she settled herself in his car again, feeling curiously carefree. It had been an eternity since she had been with a man like this, a man who made her feel giddy and feminine, young and sensual.

"Vintons," she announced. "You appreciate antiquity. It's a French restaurant in an old hotel and it's lovely. It's near Miracle Mile in the Gables."

As they drove, she allowed herself to lean back, close her eyes and smile slightly. Let it happen, she told herself. No, don't be a fool, a stern voice counseled. He was striking and strong and so sexual. She'd be setting herself up for a gigantic fall....

He liked the restaurant. As soon as they were seated, he ordered wine. Jade reminded herself to go slowly, but her first sip of wine went down so smoothly that she forgot her own advice. She found herself smiling at him, longing to flirt a bit.

"I love this place at night," she told him. "The waiters bring the ladies roses and pillows for their feet."

He gazed at her over his wineglass. "You come here often?"

She shook her head. "Dinner is very expensive. It's a special occasion type of thing."

He asked her how long she had been in her house, and she smiled, telling him that she had inherited it from her grandparents. "My grandfather was a true pioneer. As a teenager, he worked on Henry Flagler's railroad. My mother hated the old place; I loved it. She and Dad moved up to Daytona when he retired, so I inherited the house."

She asked him about his work, and was surprised when he mentioned that he had actually majored in broadcast journalism in college. She asked him if he came from Chicago originally, and learned that he'd been born in Monona, Wisconsin.

And all the while, she continued to sip her wine. She wasn't drunk, exactly, but she felt like smiling, like shruging away inhibition to ask personal questions.

"Have you always had money?" she asked him.

He laughed. "That's rather blunt. It could even be considered rude."

She shrugged. "Don't answer, then."

But that enigmatic smile was on his lips, and he moved slightly closer to her, idly running a finger over the ashtray.

"I wasn't exactly born with a silver spoon, but my dad was a fairly prosperous attorney. And yes, Mrs. McLane, I made lots and lots of money throwing that little ball around the field like a dumb jock. I know that insults your sensibilities, but I'm afraid it's the way of the world."

She stiffened slightly, but then laughed. "I asked for that one, didn't I?"

"Yes, you did."

The wine seemed to rush through her. No, that was an excuse. It was his presence that intoxicated her.

"Did it bother you much to quit playing professionally? Aren't you ever...bitter?"

He grimaced, leaning back. "Not really. I knew the moment I heard my leg shatter that it was all over. I just felt lucky to walk again." A smile played about his mouth. "And I actually was aware that there could be other things in life beside playing ball."

Jade lowered her eyes and stared at her quiche. "How long have you been divorced?"

"Two years."

She didn't care if her questions were personal, even rude. She lifted her eyes to his once again. "What happened?"

He shrugged. "The usual. Things went wrong. We just didn't see eye to eye anymore."

"Were you being a jock? Maybe running around a bit too much?"

The compression of his lips warned her that she had gone too far.

"Sure. Something like that."

He picked up his wineglass and drained it. Then he reached out and caught her hand across the table. "And what is your thing, Jade? Your husband died, so you decided you'd spend your life dwelling in memory? Have you turned him into a saint, someone mortal man could never match?"

She snatched her hand away. "We'd better go. We both have children to pick up from school."

He signaled for the check. When he pulled her chair back, he almost—almost—touched her.

She felt very stiff in his luxurious car. She knew she should keep quiet, but she seemed to be on a road to destruction that she couldn't leave.

"Isn't it strange that you have custody of Ryan?"

"No," he replied briefly, braking for a yellow light. "Diana didn't want custody. I did."

She ran her hand over the upholstery. "This is a big car for two people," she murmured.

He made an impatient little sound. "A friend of mine was killed in a compact. I like big cars—they're safer. Not like that little death trap you ride around in." He glanced her way just before the light changed. "Our cars barely connected the other day. Mine had a few scratches—yours is a mess. And the way people drive down here—"

He broke off when she stiffened all over again. "It's the Northerners who come down who don't know how to drive."

He chuckled softly. "That still rankles, doesn't it?"

"Of course."

She glanced out the window. He seemed to know where they were going well enough; he was heading east on Douglas, past Grand, ready to turn onto Main.

"Oh!" she gasped suddenly. She had been struck by an idea so wonderful, it left her breathless for a minute.

"Oh what?"

"I just thought of something."

The Harrison house was her own listing. And Jeff was so damned determined to spend money. The commission... all her own!

Commission—what a way to think of life. But she couldn't help it. She could fix her car and her roof. She would be able to go to the grocery store without trying to count the bill in her head. It Jeff really wanted to spend that much...

"What time is it?" she asked him anxiously.

"Two-thirty."

"Turn left up ahead."

"Up ahead where? All I can see is branches."

She laughed. "I know. But trust me. There's a road."

He turned into the driveway and braked quickly at her warning. Jade jumped out of the car, fumbled in her purse for the ring that held keys to the various houses she was listing and opened the high wrought-iron gate. Then she hurried back to the car.

"Drive in," she told him.

He arched a brow. "What's this?"

"A house. It's on over two acres of land. You've got tons and tons of foliage, six bedrooms, four baths. Upstairs, downstairs, pool and dock. And it's an historic landmark."

"We can see it now?"

"Yes, it's my listing. I have the keys."

They moved slowly down the curving driveway. Jade couldn't help smiling as she watched him survey the lush bushes and trees. There were crotons in a variety of colors, banyans dripping moss, hibiscus in bright red and yellow and pink.

"Is this more of what you had in mind?" she asked lightly, feeling a flush of excitement rise to her cheeks.

She could see that this was what he wanted. Lock, stock and barrel. The price of the property was more than double that of anything else she had shown him, but if he couldn't afford it, at least he'd see that he would have to lower his standards a little to buy something less expensive.

She loved the Harrison house. Somehow it had all the grace and dignity of the man who had built it.

"Stop here!" she said excitedly. "It's fun to come up the walk."

He gazed at her, not quite sure what to make of her sudden enthusiasm. But he drew the car to a halt and left it only a bit more slowly than she did. His eyes were on the coral rock portico that covered the drive just ahead. Beyond it, the house itself had four symmetrical towers, each surrounded by floor-to-ceiling windows.

"The front is gracious," she said offhandedly. "The back—well, you'll see."

She led him around the house on a path heavily laden with ferns and flowers. At the rear of the property there was a free-form pool with an island and a gazebo in the center of it. A charming bridge led to it, separating a whirlpool bath from the main body of water.

"When the whirlpool is on, it cascades like a waterfall into the pool. And there's a wonderful lighting system for night—blue and green and mauve. It's solar heated. Mr. Harrison just redid it all last year. Down there is the dock. It needs a little work, but then, you don't have a boat, do you? You could fix it in time. Back there is the guesthouse—it's all set up. But come on, you should see the house itself first."

The outer patio led into a huge entertaining center with raw rock walls, wicker furniture and a wet bar. Jade led him into the kitchen, which was large enough to contain a huge butcher-block worktable in the middle. Copper utensils hung from the ceiling, and there was a fireplace and a breakfast table with a skylight above it.

"Well?"

"I'm impressed—lead on."

"I will!"

There was a paneled library filled with books. There was a real old-fashioned bar, with stools obtained from the old Breakers hotel. There was a formal dining room that could easily seat a dinner party of twenty. The living room was huge, with floor-to-ceiling windows, gleaming hardwood floors and a wonderful old fireplace.

Jade had always loved the entryway. Its light marble flooring, domed ceiling and gracefully curving spiral staircase were spectacular.

"Still impressed?"

He grinned slightly. "Yes."

"The best is yet to come!"

Upstairs, the hallway led both east and west. The rooms were all very large, and two included window seats by the towers. Jade said nothing as she swept through room after room and led him finally to the master suite.

It occupied the entire eastern end of the house. One door led to the den, one to the bedroom itself and the two rooms were connected by a bath done in red, black and gold. The bedroom itself was huge, with white gauze drapes that would whisper in the sea breeze when the tower window was open. Velvet curtains could be lowered over the gauze in winter; right now they were pulled back, and the view of the bay beyond was breathtaking. The bed was a huge old brass one, tastefully covered with a tapestry spread. There was an entertainment center facing it, complete with television, stereo and VCR. And there was still room for a couch, a little round morning table and a refrigerator, which sat beside the bathroom door. Jade hurried through the bedroom and bathroom to show him how the den connected, then scurried back into the bedroom to stand by the window.

She barely felt him behind her as she threw open the window to the day. "Isn't it fabulous?"

She turned at last to see him watching her. He was curiously intent on her instead of the house.

"You seem to think so."

"I think it's the most beautiful place in the city," she said honestly.

"What's the price on it?"

"Two million."

His brows rose.

"It's worth it! The owner could have priced it even higher. Just the value of the land...well..." She shrugged. She hadn't really expected him to say, Oh, is that all? Write a contract.

She planted her hands on her hips and dared him with a grin. "Hey, you wanted land. You wanted water. You wanted a big house. You wanted a pool. This is it!"

"Yes, I guess it is," he answered vaguely.

He was still watching her, and she felt tense suddenly. Very tense. It was as if there were something in the air between them, something electrical. She wanted to beg him to touch her...

But she didn't. She steeled herself against the feeling, against the power in his sky-blue eyes. Against the sight of him, tall and dark and lazily powerful like a Bengal tiger.

"Well," she replied uneasily, "I guess I had better lock up and get home. I have to pick up Sean, and you have to get Ryan."

He nodded. She felt horribly disappointed as she hurried down the stairway. Not because of the house. But because she had been so certain that he was going to kiss her....

When he dropped her at her house, he said casually, "Do you have a survey on the property?"

"Yes. At the office."

"Do me a favor, if you can. Get it after you pick up Sean. I'll get a pizza and Ryan and come back, and you can tell me everything you know about it."

Jade nodded. She watched him leave in a daze. She had to shake herself before she get into her own car to go and pick up her son.

Jeff did come back, with Ryan and two pizzas and little containers of salad. After they ate, Jade showed him the legal survey and the architect's plans. She told him about the Harrisons.

"They were wonderful people. They never had any children of their own, but they were great to all the neighborhood kids. They had a party every Halloween for all of us. And Mom told me once that during the Depression, they both used to dress up like Santa

Claus and drive around with turkeys and hams and presents for anyone out of work.''

"I'd like to meet him. Think you could arrange it?"

"Sure."

She didn't know whether to be excited or not. Part of her couldn't help tallying the money she could make if Jeff bought the Harrison place. Another part of her didn't care in the least about money. She had no control over the feelings he aroused in her.

Unfortunately, his manner remained businesslike. He was friendly, but he never came close enough to touch her. He leaned against the piano when they talked. He laughed. Sometimes she felt the touch of his eyes, and the feeling was so sensual that she wanted to scream.

And yet it couldn't have been real. He made no advance. At eight o'clock, he called for Ryan and left, telling her he'd like to go out a few more times, because he wanted to see a lot of property before making a decision.

Jade agreed; they made arrangements for the following Wednesday.

The weekend came. On Sunday, Sean shouted for her to join him in the family room. She went in to find him watching Jeffrey on television. Jade didn't know much about sports, nor did she care, but she found herself slowly sinking down beside Sean and staring at the screen. Jeffrey was perfect for the job of sportscaster. He was articulate, and he had a way of speaking that made her feel as if she wanted to know what he was talking about. He was excited about his subject matter, very knowledgeable, and the camaraderie between him and the other sportscaster on the show was easy and relaxed and pleasant to watch.

Jade was still staring at the television when the show ended.

She stayed awake a long time that night, watching the ceiling in the dark, wondering if she liked the feeling of falling in love, or if the excitement and the adrenaline and electricity that she felt when he was near were actually a form of torture.

She couldn't be in love. She barely knew him!

She saw him at practice on Tuesday. He smiled at her; he talked to her. But then he talked to everyone, because everyone was talking about his Sunday sports program.

They even went to dinner again. She sat next to him, felt his thigh next to hers, the force of his gaze when he cast it her way. But nothing happened, nothing really personal.

The next morning they looked at more houses. She showed him more of Coconut Grove, more of Coral Gables, something of Pinecrest and Palmetto.

They went to lunch at a restaurant in the Mayfair, an outstanding mall in the Grove with expensive shops, exquisite foliage and fountains, marble work and tile murals.

They sat in the center restaurant, where skylights opened above them. She told him that she had spoken with Sam Harrison, and that he would be very pleased to meet Jeffrey.

She grimaced. "Even Sam likes baseball."

"Ah, yes, even Sam. But you don't?"

She shrugged. "I don't hate it." She grinned. "Stick around long enough—you'll see I'm the only parent who makes almost every practice and every game."

"Toby told me about your husband, you know."

She looked down at her food, not really knowing what to say. "It wasn't the game that killed Danny. He was..." She lifted her shoulders and let them fall. "He was entertaining the spectators. Acting the clown."

"How old was Sean when his dad died?"

"Seven."

He was pensive for a moment, then he asked, "You only wanted one child?"

She laughed a little uneasily. "No. I was an only child. It can be very lonely."

He grinned. "I know. I'm one, too."

Jade fell silent, wondering whether Jeffrey sensed her feeling of loneliness now, her longing to reach out to him. If he did, he made no motion to encourage her. When he brought her home so that she could pick up Sean, he still hadn't touched her.

It was the same story when they went out to dinner after practice the following Tuesday. But even though he made no overt advance, she knew that the other parents on the team smiled when they watched them, as if they saw more than she did. Almost as if they were a pair.

On Thursday night, Jeffrey maintained his distance, but the evening was to end quite differently from their other recent meetings. They fell into a heated argument. Ridiculously, it was over the cars again.

They were parked back to back, about ten feet apart in the small drugstore lot. Jade put her car in reverse—and the next thing she knew, she was jerking forward as a scraping sound tore through the car.

"You hit him, Ma!" Sean called out.

"I hit him—"

Jeffrey was beside her car in the next instant, pulling her door open. There was nothing casual about him now, nothing nonchalant.

"Don't you ever watch what you're doing?"

His eyes were indigo in the darkness, his features set in a grim mask. She felt both defensive and furious. It was the second damned time! And once again, his bumper was barely scratched, while the poor Corvette...

"You drive around in a death trap like that, and then you don't even watch where you're going! Dammit, Jade! Women drivers—I swear they should be outlawed on the road..."

He kept on going. He had the nerve to keep going. Mr. Jock, Mr. Muscles, Mr. Competence—going on about women drivers!

"You bastard!" she raged suddenly, heedless of the fact that both boys were hearing every word. "Why didn't you look where *you* were going? They should have arrested you the other day! They should have put you in jail! You think that just because you can throw a little ball around, you can drive! Oh! I hope they do put you in jail!"

"I'd like to wring your neck! Someone needs to take you in hand! In fact, someone should take a hand to your fanny, and I'm just about ready to do it!"

"Oh! You damned well never will!"

She gunned her car and it jerked forward, right over the low cement piece that marked the parking spot.

"Mom—" Sean began.

"Shut up! Just shut up!"

At home, she paced the living room for half an hour. Sean had the good sense to keep quiet.

The phone rang. The answering machine was on, but Jade snatched up the receiver anyway.

"Hello?"

"Jade, it's Jeffrey. I—"

She slammed down the phone. There was one benefit to being single. There was no stupid *male* to yell at her for wrecking a car, to assume that she was the one at fault just because she was female.

The phone rang again. She picked it up, ready to tell Jeffrey Martin that he and his big Lincoln could go to hell.

Unfortunately, it wasn't Jeffrey; it was Ryan, asking her in a very small voice if he could speak with Sean.

Jade released a long breath and called Sean to the phone.

Every now and then she caught him looking at her. He spoke mainly in monosyllables and laughed often. It nearly drove her crazy to discover that he usually laughed when he gave her one of his sly glances.

"Tomorrow," he said. A few minutes later he said, "Downtown." Then he added, "Oh, you know about realtors. My mom has what they call a closing tomorrow. When the buyers actually take the house from the sellers."

Jade frowned, wondering why Sean was giving Ryan a lesson in real estate. What possible interest could two little nine-year-olds have in a closing?

"Sandy, Mom's boss, was supposed to do this one. But his nephew is getting married tomorrow. It takes hours to get everything straight. Yeah, I'm sure."

He came up with a few more yeses and nos, and then hung up the phone. He stared at her very smugly, like the cat who had eaten the canary.

"What was that all about?" she demanded suspiciously.

"Oh, nothing. Ryan was just curious," Sean said innocently. He kept his eyes wide and guileless as he went on. "Ryan likes you a lot, Mom. He's afraid you're mad at him."

She took a deep breath. "I'm not mad at Ryan."

"Just at Jeff, huh?"

"Sean, go to bed."

"Sure."

But he paused. "Ryan says you're the prettiest lady he's ever seen, other than his mother."

"Oh, yes? Well, that's nice." She tried to sound casual. She chewed lightly on her lower lip. "Does he see his mother often?" She was still furious; she didn't know why she asked the question, except that she couldn't help herself.

"Not since they moved down here," Sean informed her. "But before that . . ." He shrugged. "She used to come over whenever she felt like it. He said it hurt bad when they were divorced. They got along okay after the divorce, though, and his mother even came over to stay sometimes. Maybe he hopes they'll get back together."

"Maybe they will," Jade forced herself to say with a pleasant smile. Sean grinned elusively in return, gave her a kiss good-night and walked on down the hall.

Damn him! Damn Jeffrey Martin! So he was just marking time until he got back together with his wife! Diana. Jade started to hate the name.

What did she care? He was a jerk. He was a good reason all by himself for a war between the sexes.

She was shivering with anger and some other emotion she couldn't name. She didn't know if she wanted their relationship to be over or not. Surely it would be best to get away from him now.

She was afraid; she couldn't help it. Afraid of wanting him, afraid of being in love with him, afraid of being touched again.

"I'm not even speaking to him," she muttered aloud. "So how can I fall in love with him?"

She kept talking to herself as she got into bed. She called him every name she could think of, but still she couldn't fall asleep.

"He'd better have a good apology this time," she whispered in the darkness.

On Friday morning she drove downtown to the lawyer's office for the closing. But right after she reached the law offices of Dunlap and McPherston, Sandy came in behind her.

"Sandy!"

"Take the morning off, young woman," he told her grandly.

"What are you doing here?"

"That little hothead. My nephew got into a fight with his fiancée last night and the two little twits called the whole thing off!"

"Oh. Well, better before the wedding than after," Jade said sympathetically. "But you should have taken the morning off—"

He grimaced. "The Donaldsons are my clients, and I'm here, anyway. Go home. Take a nap. You look like hell."

"Thanks a lot!"

"Well, you do. You look tired."

Jade sighed and decided that she could use a nap. She just hoped she could fall asleep.

But when she trudged back to the garage to pick up her car, it was gone.

She didn't believe her eyes at first. Then she panicked. Desperately, she searched all the levels of the garage.

It was gone. Really and truly gone.

Jade kicked the tires of a Mercedes standing next to the empty space where the beat-up Corvette should have been. Then she burst into tears. And then she called the police.

The officer was irritatingly casual. Cars, it seemed, were reported stolen all too frequently. He kept acting as if she were a feather brained woman who had probably left her keys in the car. She showed him her keys. He called in the report, chewing gum all the while and giving her very little encouragement.

"Probably won't see it again, lady," he warned her.

He was decent enough to give her a ride home. Once in the privacy of her house, she started swearing and throwing pillows around. Dammit! The Corvette was so old that she hadn't been able to insure it against theft. Why hadn't the jerk taken the Mercedes, whose owner would have made a bundle when the insurance company paid up?

She was starting to cry with sheer frustration when her phone started ringing. She ignored it; the answering machine was on.

But she couldn't ignore the voice that came on the machine. It was Toby's.

"Jade! Jade, you have to be there! Pick up the phone! Jade—listen, this is important! They've got Jeffrey Martin in the Dade County jail. Now, come on, I know you told him last night that that was where he belonged. But a joke's a joke; enough is enough, huh? Hey, he was just trying to fix the damned thing for you. Jade! Come on, pick up the phone! They've arrested him. He's in jail. Enough, okay? Jade, please pick up the phone!"

Chapter 5

Clang!

That much, at least, was just like the movies, Jeffrey mused.

He'd been in jail once before. When he was eighteen and had gotten too rowdy. But he'd been arrested by a kindly midwestern sheriff who'd taken him to wait in a comfortable room while he called his father. He'd been the only "criminal" in the jail, and the sheriff had given him a good talking to while pumping coffee into him. He'd been a kid.

He was an adult now. Responsible, dependable, mature—and humiliated as hell over this whole damned experience.

The police were very polite, and they were obviously a little bit embarrassed to be throwing him in jail. But he had been driving a stolen car, and even as he tried to explain what he was doing, they'd miserably scratched their heads and warned him that he would have to tell it to the judge.

At least they had let him make more than one phone call. He'd called his lawyer first, then Toby. Of course, the lawyer could have called Toby, but Jeffrey had wanted to hear his friend's voice himself. He needed to make certain that someone would be there to pick Ryan up from school.

Jeffrey felt the eyes of the other men in the holding tank. Someone was reaching for his wristwatch. He hardened his mouth, jabbed his assaulter with an elbow and spun around in a fury, ready to take on anyone else who wanted to cause trouble.

There were about eight men in the tank; they were all staring at him, including the bearded fellow who had grunted in pain when the force of Jeff's elbow had connected with his ribs. He didn't think he'd ever seen a more ragged lot. The cell stank to high heaven. Great. This was a wonderful, wonderful situation.

In his mind he heard Jade's words: "They should have put you in jail!"

Well, she had meant it.

Damn her, he thought for the thousandth time. She must have done this on purpose. Nine-year-old boys never kept secrets, so Sean must have given the plan away and she must have canceled her damned closing just to get to the police to report him. Women. They were all worthless! Cold and calculating. He should have known after Diana. There was just no dealing with them. He had been smart enough not to get involved after his divorce. Until Jade...

Even though he'd never touched her, they were involved. It was in their eyes, in their laughter, even in their anger. It had been in every room where they had ever stood together. He could have touched her, kissed her, on any number of occasions. It was just a matter of time. He'd wanted that time because their relationship wasn't just casual or merely physical. At the Harrison place he had felt their mutual longing like a cloak of velvet and silk around him. As he'd watched her stand before that window, the breeze ruffling her hair, her eyes bright with enthusiasm, he had wanted to touch her so badly that holding himself back was agony.

Yet he had done it. He had done it because he had a vision of the future. The relationship between them was going to be a solid one. Because she was real. He saw it when she was with the kids; he had seen it when she was working. Her laughter was real, and even her anger was real. She was flesh and blood, as natural as the earth and sky, and his faith in her had grown as deep as the initial sexual charge of desire that had first attracted him....

Damn it! Real she might be, but she was one tough customer, too! Here he was in a damned holding cell with the dregs of the earth, and all because of her! To make matters worse, the scruffy-looking men were starting to shuffle toward him.

"Ooh—eee! Will you look at that jacket, Juany, boy?"

"Juany" muttered something beneath his breath in Spanish. The men took another step forward. From somewhere in the back of the cell, an old battered drunk hiccupped loudly.

Jeff stiffened his back against the bars and narrowed his eyes. He looked at the gray-gaired geezer who had spoken first.

"Old-timer, I don't want to hurt you. Touch me, and I'll break your arm."

"He's not so big," the old guy told "Juany".

"Not so big, man? Looks tall to me. And it's not the size that matters, it's the arm!"

They were discussing him like a piece of meat. Jeff decided he'd better convince the group that he could be dangerous.

"Lean and mean, old-timer. I'm six three and I'm carrying around two hundred pounds of muscle. I'm opting for peace, but push me and you'll have a war on your hands."

The shuffling paused. They were all looking around uncertainly.

Then oddly, a grin broke out across Juany's swarthy Latin features. "Eh, man, you always get so pushed out of shape just cause a group of guys want an autograph?"

He pushed the others out of the way and stared at Jeff with a big smile on his face. "Amigos! Big, si! He's got the best right arm in the world!"

His hands were on his hips then, and he was staring at Jeff as if he were his long-lost best friend. "Roberto and me watched you on the tube! Hey, Roberto! We both watched you on the screen at Pablo's down on Biscayne Boulevard! Jeffrey Martin! Oh, man, where ever did you learn to throw a ball like that?"

"Like the Cincinnati game—"

"Did you see him in Houston?"

"California was my favorite—"

Jeff closed his eyes, gripping the bars behind him. Thank God for baseball! They didn't want to do him physical harm. All they wanted was his autograph.

"Hey, man, you are Jeffrey Martin, aren't you?"

"That's him. Yeah, ain't you seen no TV lately? He's down here doing sports shows. And I mean he is *good*. Ten times better than that pansy they had on before."

The old man stepped forward again. "Jeffrey Martin, what are you doing in jail?"

Jeff shrugged his shoulders and grinned weakly. Then he started signing the scraps of paper the men were digging out of their wallets while he answered, "Grand theft auto."

"Did you do it?" Roberto asked eagerly.

"Hell, no!" Jeffrey said with disgust. "I was trying to do a good deed for a friend, get the car fixed, and the next thing I knew, I was in here."

Another middle-aged Latin muttered something in Spanish and threw himself onto one of the bunks. Juany laughed.

"Jorge says it must have been a woman."

"Yeah, actually, it was."

Juany shook his head. "Can't trust them, eh?"

Silently, Jeff shook his head.

Maybe she hadn't done it on purpose.

She had; he was sure. Sean must have told her.

"Got a cigarette, amigo?" Juany asked.

"Sure." Jeffrey tossed the pack out. "Help yourselves."

This was going to be a long, long day. Where was his lawyer?

* * *

"You say, lady, that you reported your car stolen, but it wasn't really stolen."

"Yes, yes," Toby answered impatiently for her.

It would have to be the same cop she had reported the theft to, Jade thought miserably.

The man lowered his head over his report. "Ah, lady," he muttered, and she could just read his thoughts; feather-brained woman was what he really meant.

"Look, I'm sorry," she explained levelly. "There was a terrible misunderstanding—"

Another officer in blue came to the desk, motioning to the one who was talking with her. He stood up for a minute, then came back. "All right, the stories jibe. Just sign here. Mr. Martin's attorney is at the jail; you can go down with this waiver, and he'll be released without bond. Boy, I hope the papers don't get hold of this one. And, lady—"

"My name is Mrs. McLane," Jade interrupted smoothly.

The officer waved a hand in the air. "Lady—Mrs. McLane—we really do have a lot of that 'vice' stuff you see on the tube. Murderers and rapists and thieves and a cocaine war that would make your head spin. We haven't got time down here for lovers' spats, okay? Next time you get mad at your boyfriend, hit him over the head with a loaf of bread or something, huh?"

"He isn't my— I didn't—"

"Jade, let's go," Toby whispered insistently in her ear. "Please, please, smile nicely and let's go."

She clamped her lips together furiously and allowed Toby to lead her away from the officer's cluttered desk. It wasn't until she was seated in his comfortable Buick that she felt her wrath begin to fade and an unease that felt annoyingly like cowardice creep over her.

"Hey, Toby, maybe I should hop on the Metrorail and you should go to the jail alone. The kids will getting out of school—"

"Lynn is going for all three boys; you haven't a thing to worry about. We're almost there, Jade. Just sit tight, and we'll have Jeff out." He shook his head sorrowfully. She felt her temper explode all over again.

"I didn't have him put in jail on purpose!"

"Come on, Jade, we all heard you yelling at him the other night!"

"Yes, and I tell Sean a dozen times a week that I'm going to knock his head into a wall, and obviously I don't mean that either!"

Toby sighed and gazed at her curiously. "You mean you really didn't know that he was taking your car to get it fixed?"

"No!" She screamed the word in frustration. "How would I know? And for that matter, how the hell could you have known? What turned you into the white knight in this whole affair?"

Toby was silent as he guided the car onto the overpass. Then he glanced at her quickly. "He's been staying with us. Jeff and Ryan, that is. You didn't know that? You've been showing him houses and you didn't even know that he was staying with us?"

"No... I... I've never had a reason to call him," Jade mumbled. "Toby, I really don't want to go to the jail."

"Oh, come on. We're there."

He parked the car and put coins into the meter. Then he slipped an arm around her shoulders. "This will be a breeze. We'll just go in, find Jeff's lawyer, turn over the slip and he'll be out. We'll go home, Lynn will throw some steaks on the grill, and this whole mess will be forgotten, hmm?"

"Toby, this was not my fault."

"Okay, it wasn't. But we should clear it all up, anyway. You know, you and Jeff ought to get it all straightened out."

"I *am* getting it straightened it out. I came downtown and let that cop make an idiot out of me, didn't I?"

"But you're afraid to be here now. You're afraid of Jeff Martin."

"I am not!"

"You are!"

"Am not!"

"Good, then let's go in and get him."

"Toby—"

Too late, she realized that she was already inside the jail building. Before she knew it, she and Toby and Jeff's lawyer were standing outside the holding tank.

Jeff was leaned against one of the tawdry bunks, smoking, staring at the ceiling.

"Hey, Martin. This must be for you!" one of his cellmates said.

Then a number of them started to laugh. "That's her, huh? The one who caused all the trouble," one of the men called out.

Jade stepped behind Toby, her face turning pink. So Jeffrey Martin had sat there and complained about her to a bunch of criminals. How dared he . . .

She glared at him over Toby's shoulder. His hair was tousled, his shirt was open and his jacket was wrinkled. He looked uncomfortable and very angry.

"Mr. Martin, you're all set," the guard said cheerfully.

"Thanks," Jeff said. "Tyler—" He gazed at his attorney. "I appreciate your getting down here so quickly. You too, Toby."

A moment later he was leading the way back down the corridor. Another gate was unlocked, then one more, and then they were out on the street. Jeff's hands were on his hips; he stared up at the sky.

"I've never known the sun could feel so damned good," he muttered. Then he turned and spoke to his attorney again. Toby, Tyler and Jeff all laughed over something. Jade didn't hear what it was. She felt as if her body were on fire. He hadn't said a word to her yet.

That quickly changed. As Tyler waved and walked away Jeff spun around and bowed slightly to her.

"I've forgotten you, haven't I, Mrs. McLane? Thank you so very much for deciding to let me out of the jail I deserved to be in."

Fury seemed to rumble through her body. "You son of a bitch! Don't you dare—"

"Children! Children!" Toby interrupted, taking them both by the arm and heading toward the car. "The sun is shining, there's a delightful breeze, and all is—"

"If you start telling me all is well with the world, Tobias, I'll tear your hair out!" Jade exclaimed heatedly.

"Don't tempt her—she carries out her threats," Jeff warned.

"Now, now," Toby said. "Look—here we are at the car. We'll go home, we'll have a few drinks and something to eat and everything will be fine."

Everything wasn't fine. The first problem came as they got into the car. Not wanting to sit between the two men in front, Jade tried to crawl into the back seat.

"Take the front, Mrs. McLane. I insist," Jeff said, and his hands clamped around her waist with barely controlled strength.

"No, you take the front," she protested.

"Let's all share and share alike," Toby said in his best Little League voice, and a moment later Jade found herself in front between the two of them despite all her protests.

Jeff looked out the side window. Jade stared straight ahead. Toby drove in silence.

Jade was thankful when they drove into Toby's circular drive a few minutes later. She couldn't wait to hop out of the car and put some distance between herself and Jeff.

Toby led the way to the front door. "Hey, Lynn! We're here!" he called out cheerfully. "Where is everybody?"

Lynn came rushing out of the kitchen in jeans and a T-shirt. She had a nervously cheerful smile on her face. "Hi! Well, I'm so glad to see everyone."

"Where are the kids?" Toby asked.

"Out by the pool. Randy is with them, so they're supervised." Randy was their oldest boy, a senior at the University of Miami.

"Well," Lynn said. "Let's go out to the patio and have a drink, huh? Jade, wine?"

"Please," she said stiffly.

"Jeffrey? A bourbon?"

"Just a beer, please. But excuse me for a minute, will you? I've got to take a shower."

"Yes, yes, of course."

As soon as Jeffrey disappeared up the staircase, Jade turned to Lynn. "Listen, I really appreciate your planning to feed us all—it was thoughtful—but I really think it would be best if I just took Sean and went home."

"Jade!" Lynn protested. "Randy is always at the dorm these days; the boys are having so much fun with him. And Sean and Barry are helping Ryan and Candy with their diving. It's such a nice afternoon for them all. Please just relax." Candy was their daughter, a year younger than Barry.

Lynn didn't wait for Jade's answer, but sidled into the kitchen, which opened onto the patio.

"Lynn—"

Her hostess was already opening the refrigerator and putting a chilled glass into Jade's hand. "This is going to be so much fun! An unplanned Friday night party—with Randy in a child-watching mood . . . oh, come on, Jade!"

"I don't know if this is the right—"

"Hey, if you fall off a horse, you get right back on."

"Lynn, that analogy makes no sense! This wasn't my fault! I don't have to 'get back on' anything! I—"

"Hey, Mom!" Sean was calling her from the open sliding glass door. He was dripping wet, and wearing a delighted grin. "Did you get your car fixed?"

"Were you surprised?" Ryan asked as he appeared next to Sean.

Jade forced her mouth into the pretense of a smile. "I was surprised, all right."

"Neat! Hey, want to see Ryan dive?"

"In a few minutes, kids. Let the grown-ups unwind, okay?" Lynn said.

The boys disappeared. Someone yelled something excitedly, and Jade heard splashing water.

Toby had taken a beer and disappeared. Jade turned to Lynn. "I'm serious! Everyone is on my back, but Jeffrey Martin is the one in the wrong! Any jerk should know not to take a car—"

She was interrupted by the sound of a throat being cleared. Jade knew that it was Jeffrey.

"Lynn, I'll take that beer now, if I may."

"Ah, yes...you two go on out to the patio, okay? I've made a fondue for us to eat before dinner. Now go sit and let me play hostess."

Jade was glaring daggers at her friend, but Lynn ignored her. Taking a death grip on her wine, Jade preceded Jeffrey out to the patio. Toby was there, sipping his beer and gazing at the sports page of the newspaper. "Hey, did you read this article on the Raiders, Jeff?"

Jeff sat next to him on the divan. Jade found a seat on the other side of the patio.

Lynn came sailing in with a tray bearing a fondue pot, bread cubes, her own glass of wine and Jeffrey's beer.

"Jade, come over here, okay? We're all going to have to sit around the coffee table. Now, shape up you two!" she admonished with a laugh.

She put the tray down and sat on the tile beside the coffee table. "Jade, does this stuff taste right to you?"

Jade was obliged to sit beside her hostess and test the fondue, which was, of course, just fine. Toby commented on the warm weather; Lynn answered, and even Jeffrey roused himself to respond. But just when Jade had decided she could make the same effort, Lynn left for the kitchen again, asking Toby to come help her.

The silence on the patio was filled with tension. Jade dipped a piece of crusty French bread into the fondue; she bit into it and the sound seemed as loud as a whip crack. She felt defensive, and she didn't have to be.

She stared up at Jeff and found him staring down at her. Before she knew it, she was shouting. "Oh, come, on, Jeffrey! If your car were suddenly gone, you would have reported it, too!"

"Oh, yes. You didn't know I had the car, right?" he said, his tone seething with hostility.

"Oh, you pigheaded idiot!" she exclaimed, scrambling to her feet.

He was on his feet, too. "Sean didn't say a word, I take it?"

"No. Ask him—"

"Then what happened to your closing? That business deal that was supposed to take forever and ever?"

"Sandy came in to handle it himself. His nephew decided not to get married. This whole stinking thing is all your fault! You owe me and apology!"

He stared out at the pool area and took and a long sip of beer. His hair was damp from the shower; his shoulder muscles were so taut that they rippled beneath the blue knit shirt he wore. "I owe you an apology," he muttered. "I was trying to fix that rattletrap thing you drive—"

"I can fix my own car!"

"Ah, but you kept running around screaming that it was my fault your car was wrecked. And what about Sean? I'd just as soon not see him flattened when that thing falls apart completely. You wouldn't do anything about it though. So I decided to fix it on my own. It will *never* be a safe car, but at least the tail end won't fall off. And for my pains I got to spend the afternoon in jail with Juan and his 'amigos.'"

She moved forward to reach for his shoulder, to tell him she was sorry for what he'd gone through, but that it was still his fault. But as soon as her fingers came in contact with his bare flesh, he jerked away from her as if she were on fire.

"Don't touch me! Don't! I've spent every minute since I got out of that place trying not to touch you!"

"Oh, you are impossible!" Jade yelled at him. "Just leave my car alone in the future! Leave me alone! Then you won't have problems like you did today!"

"Hey, I think the charcoal is ready!" Lynn called out suddenly. Her timing was so good that Jade was certain she had been listening from the kitchen and had interrupted when she discovered that leaving them alone wasn't going to work as a peacekeeping maneuver.

Jeff went to help Toby with the steaks. Lynn didn't try to say anything else to Jade.

Jade called the kids out of the pool so that they could get into their clothes for dinner. Sean and Ryan were still excited about the car. Toby was the one to inform them that it hadn't been fixed. He laughed when he told them that Jeff had wound up in jail, and that they'd spent the afternoon straightening it all out.

Sean set his fork down, apparently aware of the hostility raging between Jade and Jeffrey.

"It was a neat idea, though, wasn't it, Mom? Trying to surprise you, huh? It was really nice."

Had it been a nice idea? She didn't even know. She just wanted to go home. She wasn't going to bend. Not tonight. And he was still ready to kill her.

She smiled at her son. "I think we'd better get Toby to give us a ride home, huh?"

No one protested. Jeff stayed seated. Toby drove her and Sean home, and the three of them remained dismally silent during the ride.

That night Jade slept even less than she had the night before.

There was a horn beeping out front; that was what woke her in the morning. Then she heard Sean, laughing, screaming, and throwing the front door open.

Jade rose, struggled quickly into her robe and ran barefoot out to the living room and then outside.

Jeffrey was standing there, next to her Corvette. Next to her fixed Corvette. He was leaning over the top of it, grinning, and his eyes were once again the color of a summer's day.

"Hey," he said.

"Hey," she returned, trying to smooth back her tousled hair.

He hesitated just a second. "I'm sorry."

"So am I."

"Enough to let me make some instant coffee while you get dressed? It's a perfect day. Ryan wanted to go out to the Metro Zoo. I thought I'd see if Sean wanted to come. And Sean's mother, if she felt like it. Of course, breakfast would come first."

She stood in the doorway, lowering her eyes, smiling, feeling a bit panicky at the rush of happiness that overwhelmed her.

"You—you shouldn't have had the car fixed," she told him.

"I wrecked it."

"You don't believe that."

"But you do. So how about it?"

She raised her eyes.

"Thanks."

He shook his head impatiently. "The zoo. How about the zoo?"

"Sure."

It was a beautiful day for the zoo, cool and perfect for walking. And there was a lot of walking to do, since the Metro Zoo was planned on a grand scale to give the animals vast spaces to roam in. For a long time they watched the beautiful Bengal tigers, then they saw the elephant show, and Jade taught Ryan the difference between a crocodile and an alligator. There was a special display on domestic animals, and the

boys wanted to feed the goats and sheep and don-
keys.

An overly eager goat knocked Jade down, and when
he went to help her up, Jeff found himself lying next
to her instead. Their eyes met; the kids were laughing
riotously, and the two of them found themselves first
smiling into each other's eyes, then laughing along
with the boys. It was Sean who lured the goats away
so that Jeff and Jade could stumble back to their feet.

They were loath to release each other's hands. Jade
started to follow the kids out of the paddock, but Jeff
pulled her back. He held her face between his hands
and brushed his lips against her forehead. She trembled at that light touch, and moved quickly away from
him. She was afraid of the depth of emotion she felt
at his simple gesture.

He laughed and joked and teased the kids all the
way home. When they stopped for a lobster supper
Jade tried to remind herself that he was a bad-
tempered chauvinist. But he could also be tender,
sensitive, bright, gentle, beguiling . . . and so sexy that
the sight of him filled her with a yearning hunger.

When he dropped her and Sean at their front door,
he reached for her hand, curling his fingers warmly
around it.

"Friends?" he asked her softly.

"Friends," she replied briefly. Then she ran inside,
because her heart had begun to beat like a drum, and
she was very afraid that he would hear its pounding
rhythm.

On Sunday, Jade watched Ryan as well as Toby and
Lynn's kids while Jeff worked. She made a huge pot

of spaghetti that night, and everyone ate dinner at her house.

Jeff worked Mondays, too. On Tuesday morning, they looked at houses again. That evening they all went to the drugstore for dinner.

On Wednesday morning, Jeff met Sam Harrison. On Wednesday afternoon, he came by her office— with Sam. Jade was stunned when she learned that they had come to an agreement on the price of The Grange without her even having to negotiate.

The three of them wrote up the contract together. The closing was still a month away, but there was a clause that said Jeffrey could take possession of the house that Saturday morning.

Even with the contract in her hand, Jade couldn't believe how much money she had made, or how much nicer it was going to make her life.

She was too dazed to think about much of anything. Except for Jeffrey. They'd been together so much. They'd talked, laughed, argued occasionally. And each time she'd been with him, she'd been achingly aware of him.

She couldn't think of anything to say. It didn't matter. Sam Harrison and Jeffrey had really hit it off. They were talking sports.

"See you tomorrow at practice?"

"What? Oh, yes, of course."

They were both leaving. Sam thanked her; she thanked Sam. Jeff was going to buy Sam a drink, then take him to dinner.

And she was jealous. Terribly jealous, because it meant she wouldn't be seeing Jeff that night.

Just before he walked out the door, Jeff turned to her. Sam was already out on the sidewalk waiting for him.

"Toby's having a slumber party tomorrow night," he said. "He's invited all the boys on the team."

"Yes, he, uh, has one every year."

"Well, it's perfect, don't you think?"

"For what?"

He smiled. Slowly. Lazily. His very sexy, very male, very assured smile.

"Dinner. To celebrate my buying the house. I'll take you to Vinton's and you can get your rose and the pillow beneath your feet."

"W-Who?"

"Who?" He frowned. "You and me. A date, Mrs. McLane."

Her mouth was totally dry. Perfect. The boys would both be at Toby's. Perfect . . .

"Well?"

Say yes, stupid!

"Ah, yes. It sounds . . . perfect."

Chapter 6

Late, late, late, for a very important date. All day long, Jade had felt like the white rabbit, or Alice in Wonderland herself. Things kept going wrong. Clients arrived late; sellers who were supposed to be home were not. Jade picked Sean up thirty minutes late, then rushed to get him ready for the night. Naturally, she couldn't find his good pajamas, and she didn't blame him for not wanting to go to Toby's in his old ones.

By the time they found the new pair in the dryer, it was very late indeed. It was seven when she dropped Sean off at Toby's, waved to him and Lynn and quickly drove out of the driveway, painfully aware of the Lincoln parked at the side of the house.

Back at her own house, she had less than an hour left to shower and change.

She was nervous, horribly nervous. It was only a dinner date, she tried to remind herself. But it wasn't.

It was the culmination of all the days that had gone before, all the words spoken, all the looks exchanged.

Not even the spray of the shower or the whir of the hair dryer had any calming effect on her nerves. Dinner, yes. But after dinner…she would invite him in for a drink, she would wind up in his arms, and the rest would be easy. It was all up to her…

If only she knew exactly what she wanted.

Finally, showered and dressed with five minutes to spare, Jade stood before the full-length mirror on the back of her bedroom door. She had chosen white.

Because it was virginal?

No! Because it was her best dress for the occasion. It was silk with puffed sleeves that showed off the golden tan of her arms. It had a wonderful, feminine feel to it. The skirt flowed around her when she walked, and the bodice and waist hugged her figure.

When the doorbell rang she was so startled that she actually let out a little shriek. Then she cursed herself beneath her breath, decided she definitely needed a drink and rushed to the door. Of course, she was rather breathless when she opened it and was angry with herself all over again.

He looked…perfect. His jacket was a burnished shade of brown; his trousers were several shades lighter. His hands were thrust casually in his pockets. She didn't need to touch his cheeks to know that he was freshly shaved. He smiled slowly.

"May I come in? Am I too early?"

"No! I mean, yes, come in. No, you're not early."

She felt as if her heart were sinking to her toes. Already she was as flustered as a high school senior going out with the team quarterback. This wasn't going to do at all.

"Would you like a drink?"

"Sure."

Would he like a drink. Why had she asked that? She still didn't have anything in the house except for beer and wine.

"Ah—burgundy?

"Fine."

Jade fled into the kitchen. Her fingers wouldn't work right when she tried to remove the cork. The cork crumbled and she swore softly, reached for her strainer. Not an elegant way to pour wine. Where was her sophistication?

"Let me do that for you."

Jade spun around. She hadn't heard him come into the kitchen behind her. And she didn't like the knowing, subtle smile on his lips. He knew that she was a wreck.

She smiled thinly in return, arched a brow, handed him the wine and moved several steps away, crossing her arms over her chest. "Please," she muttered.

She felt hot and feverish all over again as she watched his fingers, watched their expertise with the bottle, the strainer and the wineglasses. He handed her one, and she took a long swallow. The wine was very good; it was bottled courage.

What was she so nervous about? It was just dinner. And sex. Lord, she had every *right* to be nervous. It was a major step for her. But she would do it. She would have to, or resign herself to a life of celibacy and loneliness. For all Jeff's temper, and the maddening mockery of his smile, there were few men with his sensitivity. It was now or never.

He sipped his wine, watching her. "How was your day?"

"Hectic. How was yours?"

"I'm not sure. I spent it thinking about tonight."

There it was again, the heat, the fever, burning through her. Was it his words, or the way he had said them? She felt hot, yet the color drained from her face. He had turned back to the counter to collect the little pieces of cork scattered there, but she could have sworn he was smiling.

Jade began to chatter in an attempt to diffuse her nervousness. She talked about Sean, about Ryan, about the office, about the Grange. She finished her wine, idly poured herself another glass and kept talking. Jeffrey answered her in short sentences that barely registered in her mind. She was so aware of him that it was painful.

"Want to come with me tomorrow to christen the place?" he asked her.

"Pardon?"

"The movers can't come until Sunday—I've got some furniture, and clothing, of course, at Toby's. But I want to go over around noon tomorrow and decide what I'm going to do. I thought I'd get some champagne and we could toast the Grange."

"Ah—"

"Toby and Randy and his friends are taking the kids to the ice cream parlor for lunch at noon. Then they're going back to the house to swim for a while. You don't have to worry about Sean. Want to join me? You're the one with the talent for renovation. I'd pick you up about eleven."

"I'd pick you up...

Didn't he plan to seduce her tonight and stay at her house? Was he trying to throw her off guard by implying that nothing would happen between them?

"Sure," she said casually. "Eleven sounds fine."

He glanced at his watch. "We'd better go."

Jade nodded. The sooner they got on with this the better. She set her empty glass down and fled the kitchen. Then she practically ran out the front door.

Jeff followed more slowly. "Don't you want to lock it?"

"What? Oh."

She wanted to kick him. The color flooded back into her face as she returned to the door to lock it. Damn him a thousand times over! He knew she was a wreck. Did he intend to seduce her? Did he know the things that were going on in her mind? Did he sense her uncertainty? Was he completely confident that he could overcome her fears?

He opened the car door for her, but didn't put out a hand to help her in. As he drove, he commented on the warmth of the weather and on how nice it was not to have to buy snow tires. Jade leaned back against the plush headrest. She felt the thrum of the car's engine and found it soothing. The stereo was on, playing a soft, romantic melody. She was aware of those things, but most of all, she was conscious of Jeffrey beside her. She could reach out, place her hand on his knee. She could lean toward him as he drove, laugh, tease, flirt, do a dozen little things....

And he was talking about snow tires. Both his hands were on the steering wheel. She could see the line of his profile, and it was striking and handsome and somewhat hard all at once. She liked the look of his shoulders beneath his jacket; she wanted to touch the fabric, to feel the vitality of his body beneath it.

She didn't move. She let the subtle magic of his scent and the music wash all around her and wished that she were not a coward.

When they reached the restaurant, he opened the car door for her. As they entered the dining room, he put his arm around her so that his hand rested lightly on her hip. They were led to a table on the patio. The night was just right for dining outside, and the patio seemed so intimate with the stars above them and foliage surrounding them. Jade was handed a rose, and a pillow for her feet to rest upon. While Jeffrey ordered wine, she found herself just smiling and playing with the rose set before her.

"Do you like it?" she asked him a little shyly.

"I've been here before," he reminded her.

"But for dinner?"

"It's perfect. I like the stars, I like the plants...I like the company."

They ordered the chef's special, which could only be ordered by two. There was an appetizer of tiny white shrimp in a creamy wine sauce, salads of carrots, radishes and bamboo shoots that were as beautiful as they were delicious. Then there was a taste of scrod and oysters, sherbet to cleanse their palates, and a main course of minted lamb. All during the meal they talked of casual things, baseball and broadcasting, real estate and furniture, schools and roads and the city itself.

It was easy, Jade discovered, very easy. She kept sipping the wine, and her smile became a permanent, whimsical curve to her lips. She was so relaxed, and so comfortable that his eyes, dark blue with the night and speculative upon her, did nothing but make her feel a delicious shiver of heat again and again. When Irish coffee had been ordered and Jeff leaned back casually to light a cigarette, she didn't even stiffen as he asked her about her marriage.

"So, Mrs. McLane, what is it with you? Was your relationship with your husband so perfect that you've given up on trying to find a man to take his place?"

She didn't take offense at his tone. She just smiled nostalgically, because she had loved Danny.

"No."

"No?"

Her smile widened and she found herself playing with her rose again. "I loved Danny. Very much. But if he had lived, we wouldn't have been married today."

"Really? Why not?"

She hesitated, then shrugged. "Danny was a wonderful man. He was fun, talented, charming. Too charming. He always wanted to come back to me—but he liked to wander, too. We were separated when he died. I was at the game that day because we had talked about getting back together. But I'm not a sharer, not when it comes to marriage. I can see now that it wasn't really *in* Danny to change. Not in his *nature*." She fell silent, taking a long sip of wine and wondering why she had said such a thing to Jeff. She didn't wait for a reply, but tossed her head back and asked, "What about you, Mr. All-star Martin? How could any woman—the mother of your child, at that—be persuaded to leave you?"

He lowered his head; she didn't see his grimace or his secret grin at her epithet.

"I filed for the divorce, Jade. But when I did, Diana was already gone."

Jade brought the petals of the rose to her cheek. Jeffrey watched her, enthralled. There was something so soft and sensual, so feminine about her movements that his whole body tightened.

He knew that she was trying a little desperately to decide what she wanted. And he knew that she wanted him. It wasn't an egotistical thought. They were simply right for each other in a very special way. But she didn't quite have the nerve to admit it. She wanted the wine and the night and the stars to be her courage, and the ache within him was so strong that in certain moments he didn't really care how she came to him . . . as long as she did.

But at other moments he knew that wouldn't be enough. He wanted everything. He wanted her emerald eyes to meet his without the haze of wine, with a look of honest longing that matched his own. Another time it wouldn't matter at all. But not the first time. He wanted her as he had envisioned her once, standing before the tower window in the Grange, shedding her clothing, naked and honest in the sunlight. He wanted their ultimate joining to be perfect. Falling in love was more than the urgency of desire. This relationship was worth the wait, even if it did mean one damned miserable night.

She was still playing idly with the flower. Her hair spilled around her shoulders, golden against the white of her dress. She was beautiful in a way Diana could never even imagine.

"Your wife left you?" she asked him dubiously.

"Mmm." Her breasts were driving him crazy as they rose and fell slightly with every breath. Full and firm, they were just visible where the neckline of her dress bared her flesh. Her throat was wonderful, slim and long, its tiny pulse beats hinting at her vitality. He was never going to make it through this night. He didn't think he could wait until they got out of the restaurant to grab her and rip away her clothing....

"Maybe she couldn't take the pressure. You know— ball players. Traveling, trips—women. Groupies. Maybe you'll get back together."

"What?" Jeffrey frowned and gave himself a shake. All he could think about was her naked flesh, and she was busy getting him remarried to Diana.

"Your wife. Maybe you'll get back together."

"Never," he said harshly. The waiter was nearby. Jeff signaled for the check.

"Are you friendly?"

"Do I talk to her, do I see her? Yes. And as long as we're not married, I can be perfectly civil."

"Where does she live?"

"Wherever she feels like living. At the moment, Chicago. She moves like lightning."

"Ryan hopes—"

"We will never remarry."

"You sound bitter."

"Not bitter. Just adamant."

Adamant. He meant it. At least he thought he meant it. What was the truth? Jade wondered.

Jade tried to laugh casually. "Oh, is anyone ever sure? Maybe she'll waltz by one day and look so beautiful that—"

"Diana has always been very beautiful," he replied coolly. "It really doesn't have a damned thing to do with love or marriage."

Jade hesitated just a second, then shrugged. She wanted the truth and she was willing to take a gamble to find out where she stood.

She lifted her Irish coffee to him in a little salute. "I understand via the boys' grapevine that you and Diana have gotten back together any number of times."

He didn't blink. He continued to stare at her the same way he had been doing, except that now his eyes appeared almost black, his jaw had tightened, and his knuckles whitened as he clenched the handle of his cup.

"Just what are you asking?"

If she had any sense, she'd retreat. There was something so menacing about his quiet tone...she was almost frightened of him. But her head was spinning, and she had to have answers, even if she didn't like them.

She stared down into the whipped cream melting in her cup when she spoke. No amount of wine could have brought her to meet his eyes at that moment.

"Have you slept with her since your divorce?"

"Yes."

Well, she had insisted, and she had gotten an answer she didn't want. It hurt, and it was more humiliating than she had expected. She felt suddenly as if she wanted to get away. She reached for her purse, not really knowing what she intended to do.

He caught her wrist before she could stand. His grip was so tight that she couldn't budge his fingers any more than she could break a chain of steel. She stared at him, ready to make a trembling protest. But she never said the words. He just kept talking as if he weren't forcing her to sit still, as if he were exerting no effort.

"I've slept with her a couple of times since then. The last occasion was a long time ago. I wasn't dating anyone else at the time. What else did you want to know, Jade? Dates and places? I'm sure you've got my life down fairly pat. Let's get on to yours. There hasn't been a hell of a lot in it, has there? What did your husband do—cheat? Is that why you've tried and convicted me of the same crime? Well, I'm sorry, you're wrong."

She lifted her chin to him. "I'm wrong to judge you? Maybe—and maybe not. Danny cheated, but he always came back, even at the end, when we were thinking about a divorce. Maybe you'll always go back. Maybe Diana will always want you to come back. And maybe you won't be able to resist."

"Oh, God," he groaned. "Are you saying that because you couldn't resist? Because you always went back to Danny?"

She whitened but took another sip of her wine and said levelly, "Maybe. And maybe it's because I've seen a few too many things in my lifetime."

"*Do* enlighten me."

"All right. A friend of Toby's was dating this lovely girl. The guy was head over heels in love with her. He couldn't take a vacation; she could. He made arrangements for her to spend a week at one of the resorts and while she was there, she ran into her ex-husband. She *re*married him a *month* later."

Jeff shrugged. "Things like that do happen. They still aren't the norm."

"I don't know," she replied primly. "It's just hard as hell to trust men with ex-wives."

"All right," Jeff said blandly. "I'm untrustworthy. That's what you want to believe, isn't it?"

"No—"

"Yes, it is, Mrs. McLane. You're desperately searching for a reason not to get involved with me, but it isn't going to work. And your other little scheme isn't going to work, either."

She didn't know if she was furious, mortified, hurt—or ready to kill. She could feel his fingers as if they were steel twined around her, and she wanted to run away from him, from her own feelings. She was falling in love with him, and she knew so little about his past, his passions. She was so afraid of being hurt.

"What scheme?" she asked.

His fingers tightened their grip on her. "Your attempt to delicately sip your way into oblivion. 'Lay me down and do what you will.' This hiding and denial. You want to wake up in the morning and say, 'That wasn't so bad; I don't really remember a thing, but I did it, I went to bed with a man besides my husband.'"

She gasped and went dead still. If her arm had been free she would have hit him.

"You egotistical maniac," she breathed. "You—"

"You've been trying to seduce me all evening in your backward little way, Mrs. McLane. You—"

"Backward! Seduce you! Let go of me! I'm—"

"You're not going anywhere. You're going to calm down, and then I'm going to take you home."

She felt as if she was choking. She was furious, but her voice came out in an annoying whisper. "I'll call a cab."

He tossed money on the table with his free hand and rose smoothly, dragging her right along with him.

"I'll scream!" she threatened.

"Go right ahead."

Of course she didn't. There were too many other people there. The place was just too nice, too sophisticated, too damned French. She would have been embarrassed to cause a scene.

Her head was reeling. She wanted to strike out at Jeff so badly. Yet at the same time she wanted to touch him, to feel his hair beneath her fingers, to touch the fingers that held her so securely.

He released her at the car.

"I can take a cab," she repeated.

"Get in."

It was not a question; it was a command that was accompanied by a none too gentle shove.

He drove home in silence. She sat as stiff as a poker beside him. It wasn't a long drive from the Gables to the Grove, just a short distance down Douglas to Main, over to Park and then into her drive.

Jade meant to jump right out of the car. She planned to thank him for dinner and slam her way into the house.

But it didn't happen that way. He was out of the car before she was, at her side before she could reach the door.

"Go home!" she shouted at him.

"I'm going—as soon as you're in the house."

"I know how to open a door, dammit! Just—"

"Open it, then, and get in."

She managed to unlock the door and step inside. But she wasn't able to slam the door. He caught it with his hand. He was smiling grimly, and she felt a shiver of confusion go through her. She could have sworn he was looking at her with desire. From his expression she would have thought that he was mentally undressing her. Despite his anger, there was a certain tenderness in his eyes.

"I'll be here at eleven in the morning."

"Don't bother—"

"I'll be here. Be ready."

"Don't—" But her voice was already weak.

"Eleven, Jade. Close and bolt the door. I won't leave until I hear the lock."

She did slam the door then. She muttered that he was a macho jerk and slid the bolt home with as much force as she could.

Then she heard his footsteps receding down the walk, and she slammed a fist furiously against the door. The only thing that accomplished was to give her a stinging pain in her hand.

Anger carried her into her bedroom. It was with her when she scrubbed her face and teeth with a vengeance, with her still until she crawled into bed. Then she became morose and started to cry. She muttered out loud that he should be strangled.

Then she beat up her pillow...because she knew that she would be ready to go with him at eleven.

Jeff didn't really know what to expect when he parked the Lincoln in her driveway the next morning. He was afraid, and he didn't like the feeling of being afraid. His hands were damp on the steering wheel. Long before he reached her door his heart was pounding and he felt the nagging urge for a cigarette. It was so much easier not to care.

He rang the bell and shoved his hands into his pockets. Maybe he had been wrong last night. Maybe he should have kept his mouth shut and given in to his desires.

No. He was too old for games, too involved with this woman for anything less than an emotional as well as a physical commitment. If she came to him with no subterfuge, he would be sure that she was ready to make that commitment.

Right now, he wasn't sure about anything. Maybe she wasn't going to open the door. Dammit; he had been a fool. He should have let her drink another half a bottle of wine, curl into his arms and awake beside him. At least he would have been inside the house, instead of standing on her doorstep, aching to hold her. Maybe he was a macho bastard, he reflected dryly, but he wanted to make her a part of him, make her see that their relationship could work.

Open the door, Jade. Come with me. If you don't, I may very well break the door down and prove just what an animal I am by ripping your clothing from you piece by piece. All last night I kept seeing you ... your eyes, your hair, your golden skin....

She opened the door. She was wearing a cool halter dress, and her hair flowed freely about her naked shoulders. Her legs were bare of stockings and beautifully tanned; her feet were encased in high-heeled sandals. She seemed cool and remote, but at least she had answered the door.

"Good morning," he said, stepping inside before she could decide not to let him in.

"Good morning," she returned coolly. "Do you want coffee?"

"If you've got it made."

"It's in the kitchen. Help yourself."

She disappeared down the hall toward her room. He was tempted to follow her.

He went into the kitchen, poured himself coffee and lit a cigarette. She joined him a second later with a shoulder bag in her hand.

"How are the boys doing?"

"Fine. They've just started waking up—they watched Boris Karloff movies until 3:00 a.m."

She nodded vaguely. "I guess they're having a good time."

"Very."

"Toby and Lynn don't need any help?"

"Lynn is retiring for lunch. I told you. Toby and Randy are taking the kids to the ice cream parlor."

"Oh, yes. I'd forgotten."

"Are you all right?"

"Am I all right?"

"No hangover?"

"I didn't drink that much," she said, her tone icy.

"Sorry. I just wanted to make sure you didn't have a headache."

"How considerate," she retorted sarcastically.

"Let's go," Jeff said abruptly.

His strides took him quickly out of the house; he was afraid to see if she was following him.

But she did follow him. She slid silently into the Lincoln when he opened the door for her. As they drove, she stared straight ahead, primly adjusting the hem of her dress over her knees.

Well, this is just great, Martin, he scoffed at himself. You take a cold shower like a monk when she's ready to float into space with you, and try to seduce her when she'd like to slit your throat. What a way with women.

At the Grange, it was he who hopped out to open the gate. He motioned to her to drive the car through. She frowned, then uneasily slipped over to the driver's seat. She continued to frown as she drove the car to him.

"What ... ?"

"Go ahead. I want to walk."

"Are you sure you want me driving your car?"

He grinned. "Yeah, I'm sure. I don't think you can hit anything in a driveway."

The electric window closed in his face. She made a point of gunning the motor.

Jeff worked at getting control of himself as he walked past the wild and beautiful foliage that lined the drive. Go slowly, he warned himself.

She was waiting for him at the door. He grinned again and opened it. He led the way straight into the kitchen.

Jade hovered behind at the entrance.

"Hey! Come in here!" he called to her.

Humph! Jade thought. He was acting as if nothing had happened. Nonetheless, she found herself following him into the kitchen.

He was standing in front of the open refrigerator. He turned around with a bottle of something and two frosted glasses.

"What's this? I got the distinct impression last night that you felt I had drunk too much," Jade said.

He glanced at her, arching a brow. "This is Dom Perignon—to christen the house. And I didn't say that. I doubt that you ever really get drunk. I said that you were looking for oblivion." He poured the champagne and handed her a glass, then lifted his own in a toast. "To the Grange."

She lifted her glass to meet his. "To the Grange," she mumbled.

He sipped his champagne. "You know," he said softly, "Lynn thinks we're having an affair."

Jade choked on her champagne. "Does she?" she managed in a strangled gasp. "And does she think that you're after whatever you can get?"

"I don't know. Maybe she thinks that you're after my money," he answered pleasantly. "Are you?"

"Don't be absurd," she snapped, turning away. "What did you want me to look at?"

"Come this way, madame, and I'll show you."

He led the way to the hall and went upstairs. Jade followed him nervously. It was starting again. The heat...the shivers...the anticipation. The trembling, the wondering...

She clenched her fists. He was playing with her. He didn't want her at all; if he did, he wouldn't have left her at her door last night.

He was in the master bedroom, and she joined him there. He pointed to the tower window. "I was thinking about putting in a window seat. A period type thing. What do you think?"

Jade walked to the window. It was open; a soft, cool breeze was fluttering the drapes.

"Do you really care?" she asked him.

"Yes."

She stared out the window. "I think it would be lovely. Is that all you wanted to ask me?"

"No."

"Then what?"

"I want to know if you want to sleep with me, Jade. Now. Here. Today."

Chapter 7

Well?"

Cool air wafted over Jade's face, and the white draperies shivered in the breeze. She tried to continue staring out the window, but she couldn't. It was as if he had the physical power to force her eyes to his.

He was standing across the bed from her, his hands on his hips. Her heart started to thud painfully against her chest. She made a little movement, gave an almost inaudible gasp. Then she forced herself to shrug and smile at him mockingly.

"That...was...a little blunt, wasn't it? I mean, most people start out with a kiss. Or a dance, maybe." Her lips were so dry her palms so clammy. "We've, uh, never even held hands."

He moved around the edge of the bed. His hair seemed very dark that morning. His eyes were bluer than indigo. The plaid shirt he wore was open at the neck.

In just seconds he might be taking it off, sliding out of the jeans that hugged his form....

"Did you want that?" he asked her softly his eyes challenging hers. "The games, the play, and the flowery phrases? A slow seduction step by step?"

"I—"

Totally at a loss for words, she stared down at her hands. Then she stared at him ready with a challenge of her own.

"I don't even know if you're serious—"

"I'm very serious."

She shook her head, confused. "Last night...dinner. I—" She paused, then her temper flared, brought to the boiling point by the terrible fear that he didn't really want her, that he had somehow found her lacking.

"I think you're crazy. I would have been a wonderfully easy mark last night! I was flying like a kite! You didn't even touch me. And now here we are, in broad daylight, and you ask if I want to sleep with you as if you were suggesting a movie!"

He smiled then, his dark lashes flickering down over his eyes for a moment. "Jade, the fact that you were flying like a kite is exactly why I didn't touch you. I didn't like your attitude."

"My attitude!"

"Umm. I had this feeling that you'd decided on an experiment. It was as if you were thinking, 'I suppose I have to enter the world of the living somewhere. If I drink enough, surely I can crawl into bed with a man again. And this seems to be a pretty good specimen.

All the limbs are there, no rotten teeth, and he even has all his hair left.' "

"Oh, stop it. You're awful!"

He shook his head. "Honest, Jade. That isn't awful. I wanted it to happen in broad daylight. I wanted you sober. I wanted you to know exactly what you were doing. I wanted to ask you an honest question, and so help me, I want an honest answer. You know exactly what you feel by now. Do you, or do you not, want to sleep with me?"

Her eyes lowered. She was trembling. She could tell him no, and he would accept it. They would walk back into the kitchen and maybe finish the champagne and he would take her home.

But that wasn't what she wanted at all. She was dying for the touch of his hands, longing to lie down beside him. She had thought of little else since she had met him, yet it seemed so awfully hard to admit that she desired him. Why couldn't he have made it easy, lulled her into bed, saved her from . . . honesty?

"You, uh, haven't made things particularly easy," she commented.

"Easy isn't always best, Jade."

"I—"

Oh, thank God . . . he was going to help. Long strides brought him to her. His fingers, strong and tense, closed around her shoulders. His eyes were wonderfully persuasive when they met hers, and when he spoke his voice was deep and rough with passion.

"Do you really need the flowery phrases? I don't want to use them, but I can give you more honesty. That first day at practice I kept staring at you. And every time you moved, I tried to remove your clothing in my mind. Rip it off. I tried to figure out what it was about your eyes that held me as fascinated as a kid. What it was about your hair that made me long to touch it. At your house that night, I shook like a leaf. It was all I could do to keep from attacking you, sweeping you into my arms. I almost forgot everything but the urge to have you. No, not have you, make love to you. Because that's what I want it to be, Jade. An act of love. Not some physical experiment for which you have to be half loaded. I want you. I want to touch you, caress you, embrace you...love you. But only if you want it, too."

She could only stare at him stunned by his vehemence. She was shivering with anticipation.

"Here?" she breathed. "Now?" The word was a bit of a squeak.

He smiled slowly. "Here. Now."

"What if—"

"Harrison said the place was mine as of today, Jade. The movers will be coming in tomorrow. The front door is locked. No one is going to disturb us."

"Uh—"

"Well?"

She closed her eyes and leaned against him. "You've never even kissed me," she mumbled against his chest.

"I can rectify that."

"Please, will you?"

He caught her chin and lifted her head. His mouth came down over hers and she thought that simple action was the most erotic she had ever known. He was all the warm and wonderful things that she had thought he would be...and more. His kiss was explosive, full of hunger and longing. He was demanding as if they had been lovers always, yet he was tender, too, as his tongue learned each secret of her mouth. His touch overwhelmed her senses. She felt each stroke of his tongue throughout her body. Sweet spirals of sensation swirled through her limbs. She laced her fingers around his neck, loving the coarse dark hair at his nape. She was alive and strong with longing, weakened with the thrill of fantasy rewarded. He was warm and wonderful, and she savored the feel of his tongue in her mouth, the brush of his thumbs, the wonder of his arms.

Gently, he broke away from her, and she began unbuttoning his shirt at the cuffs. But when her fingers moved to the buttons on his chest, she hesitated and flushed slightly.

"May I?"

"Please," he said. She couldn't meet his eyes, but found fascination in the work of her fingers. Her fascination grew when the tailored plaid shirt fell to the floor. She leaned against the wall of his chest, pressed her lips to his flesh, delighted in the feel of the little dark hairs tickling her flesh.

For a moment he put his arms around her and held her there. She felt the tempo of his heart, like an ancient beat, bringing music to her blood. It was wonderful just to be held there, just to feel his arms around her. And then it wasn't quite enough, and her lips touched him like hummingbird wings, kisses that brushed his throat, his shoulders, his collarbone. His breath quickened; she heard it catch in his throat, felt him shudder as his arms tightened around her.

And then he was holding her away from him again, smiling into the confusion in her eyes.

"My turn," he told her huskily. "I want our loving to be just as I envisioned it the first time I saw this room. You...here...in front of this window. With the sun pouring in, catching the light in your hair." His hands were at her nape, moving on her zipper. The long, *zzzzz* sound sizzled through her.

The simple silk halter dress fell to the floor with a whisper. She started to murmur something, to move toward him. He shook his head, and his intense gaze, filled with both tenderness and fervor, halted her.

He knelt before her and removed her sandals, tossing them aside one by one. Then he rose, a presence that blotted out the sun, the sky, and the day beyond the window. She smiled, mesmerized.

His fingers found the hook of her bra, released it, and brushed against her breasts. She shuddered at that light contact; her breath caught as the bra fell to the floor. His fingers moved beneath the band of her slip and bikinis, taking them from her with an unhurried grace that left her both naked and so keenly aware of her own flesh that his slightest touch could bring a cry to her lips. She longed to hurl herself against him, to hide herself, to give herself, to bury herself within him.

"No..." he said softly, and his hands moved to her hair, spreading it over her shoulders. "You...here...in front of this window. The sun in your hair, pouring over your body. The very first time I was in this room, that was all I could see."

"Ohhh..." she whispered. The breeze from the open window fluttered the sheer gauze drapes, played against her skin, so cool when she was so hot. "Please . . . Jeffrey . . ."

"Umm," he murmured, and he lifted her up and carried her the few steps to the bed. He lay down beside her, leaning on an elbow so that he was slightly above her. He smiled at her, his long fingers sliding gently between her breasts, stroking her bare ribs and belly.

"I'll never forget that night when I came to your house and you were wearing that exquisite robe with the deep V neck. All I could think about doing was touching you." His hand came to her breast, the palm resting over the nipple, the fingers curling in an embrace. "Touching you, tasting you. Holding you in my mouth." His hand moved to cup her breast. His dark head lowered, and his mouth closed around her nipple.

Heat tore through her, and she cried out. Her fingers knotted in his hair, and she shuddered in reaction. Was it the long wait that made it so very sweet? Or was it his expertise, or his tenderness and honesty?

His knuckles skimmed over her stomach as his mouth moved in a more demanding caress. His hand grazed the heart of her desire, and she shuddered again. He moved on to stroke her thighs, leaving her quivering.

Her fingers left his hair to travel over the taut muscles of his shoulders and back. They found the waistband of his jeans and probed just beneath it, silently pleading that he should be as naked as she was herself. He stood, no laughter about his mouth now, just a tautness that spoke of desire gone too long unfulfilled.

She watched as he kicked away his shoes, then reached for his belt buckle with both hands. He stripped away his jeans and briefs in an easy action that had her heart slamming against her chest. She was a little afraid and totally fascinated.

It had been so easy to imagine a lover, imagine his kiss, his arms around her. But now he was real, a man of flesh and blood and pulsing life. She had never imagined she would feel this kaleidoscope of emotion: the longing to touch him, the hesitancy, the sense of wonder that in moments they would be lovers.

She was shaking as he came back down beside her. He touched her easily. One hard leg was thrown over hers, his palm rested upon her belly, and his eyes, indigo with passion, were fixed on her face.

Her fingers entwined nervously with his where they lay against her. "You've...had a lot of experience."

"Some." He kissed the pulse point in her throat, then her forehead, and the lobe of her ear. "But never like this."

She believed him. He was being absolutely honest with her.

He raised their entwined fingers and his hand tightened around hers.

"It's been a long time?" he whispered.

It didn't occur to her to be anything but honest.

"Two years. Not since...Danny. And never before Danny. I'm afraid I'm not very experienced."

A smile touched his lips, but his words were as gentle and tender as his touch.

"I can rectify that...."

His mouth claimed hers again, hard and forceful, eliciting a sweeping passion within her. The passion took flight within her, swirling and spiraling and growing until it was all she knew. She felt the hardness of his leg against hers, the knotted tension in his body. His hand was constantly moving, stroking her breast, her hip, her thigh. It came to the juncture of her legs and invaded with the same sureness his tongue had shown in the moistness of her mouth. The bold rhythm of his touch sent her arching against him, gasping at the sensation.

His mouth left hers and buried itself in her throat. He uttered things that made no sense to her, for she had never felt so delirious, so desperate to ease the want, the emptiness, the need for him.

"Oh, God, Jade, I've got to have you. Now. I—" His mouth found her breast, adding even more fuel to the fire that consumed her. "I meant to wait, to play, to touch every inch of you."

He slid down her body, between her knees and parted them gently. Where she was so keenly sensitive, he touched her with the passion of his kiss. The sensation that followed was so sweet that tremor after tremor racked her. She tried to wrench herself away, alarmed at the flood of ecstasy that swept over her like an incoming tide.

But then his arms were around her again, and the rock-hard length of his body was against hers. She dared to open her eyes, to meet his determined gaze. Briefly, she touched her tongue to her lips; then his were there again. The kiss rocked them wildly.

In the next moment he was entering her, exploding into her with a thrust that filled her body with wonder. She closed her eyes. Her body moved with his. Moved and moved.

She seemed to explode all over again, and this time the explosion left her so completely sated and tranquil that it was long moments before she drifted back to reality. She was damp with the sheen of exertion, shivering from the force of their lovemaking. And try as she might, she could not convince herself that they had only made love, like billions of men and women before them. She was convinced that nothing had ever been like this, nor could anything ever be quite like this again.

"Oh" was all she could whisper. She tucked her head into his chest, hiding there as he chuckled softly, gliding his fingers over her hair, holding her close.

But he didn't let her hide for long. He slid down the bed so that his eyes were level with hers. His thumb stroked her cheek. "I'm sorry. I meant to be slow and completely seductive, the most giving lover you could ever encounter. The fantasy got the best of me. I'd imagined you before that window and then in my arms so many times that when I really touched you, I thought I die if I couldn't be a part of you right then."

Jade felt suddenly shy all over again, stunned at the depth of their intimacy. She blushed as she remembered each erotic moment.

Her lashes lowered. "I...I don't think I could have handled anything more. I've never felt quite like this. So close to dying if I didn't reach something, so close to heaven when I did."

He laughed, but there was such honest pleasure in it that she couldn't be offended. "My God, babe, are you a sweetheart. But I promise, I'm going to make it up to you."

She spoke in a muffled voice, her mouth half buried in the pillow. "You! But I...I barely touched you. I—"

"I didn't give you much of a chance. But feel free anytime. I plan to give you lots and lots of opportunities."

"Jeff," she whispered, opening her eyes and staring at him with the awe she was feeling.

But then they both started, because the phone rang, right next to the bed. The loud noise seemed to destroy the intimacy of the moment.

Jade sat up, drawing the spread around her as they both frowned.

"Who would be calling?" she asked.

"I guess anyone might have known we'd be here," he muttered, reaching for the receiver, totally relaxed in his nakedness.

"Hello?"

"Who is it?" Jade asked.

He didn't answer her. Whoever it was had brought a very pensive look to his features. A frown tightened his brow; his jaw grew hard. The pulse beating in his temple now had nothing to do with passion, and everything to do with anger.

Still, when he spoke, his voice was even and controlled.

"Thanks, Toby. I appreciate your calling, and I'm glad you thought of the house. What? I'd say that I've moved in as of today. Yes, she's here. No, no. I am glad. I'll handle the situation." His eyes flickered over to Jade for a second, but she felt that he wasn't really seeing her.

Then, even while he was still talking, there came another sound that startled them both.

The front door opened and slammed.

"I thought you said you locked the door!" Jade exclaimed.

"I think she's here now, Toby; I've got to go."

Jeffrey hung up the phone, looking very grim. Immobilized by shock and confusion, Jade watched as he reached for his briefs and jeans. Only slowly did it occur to her that he knew who had just entered the house and that the "who" was a "she."

She muttered something that didn't bear repeating and dashed for her clothing just as the woman's voice drifted upstairs.

"Jeffrey? Jeff—are you here?"

Jade was mortified and burning with fury. She couldn't get her bra hooked. Jeff tried to help her, but she jerked away, staring at him with an accusatory glance.

"Look, I didn't—"

"Don't *touch* me. Who...? Put your shirt on!"

But he didn't seem very concerned about his shirt. "Jade, dammit, I didn't plan this. I had no idea she was in town."

"*Who?*"

"Diana."

Diana. His ex-wife was downstairs, for heaven's sake. No, she was coming up the stairs.

She managed to get into her clothes in thirty seconds flat. Her sandals were still lost somewhere, the bed looked undeniably tousled, and dammit, so did she. As for Jeffrey, he didn't seem at all concerned that his shirt still lay on the floor and that they were both barefoot. He seemed angry, nothing more. Clearly, he was not about to hide his activities.

"Jeffrey...?" The soft, melodic voice floated to them once more, and then she was there, standing in the doorway.

She was beautiful. Stunning. Her hair was almost jet, sleek and stylish with fluffy bangs that complemented the perfect oval of her face. She had the darkest, most alluring eyes Jade had ever seen. Her casual blouse and three-quarter-length slacks might have come right off a page of *Vogue*. And she was *built*. Oh, was she built. She had high breasts, a tiny waist and long legs.

How could I ever compete? Jade wondered, and she wondered at the same time how she had ever allowed herself to fall into bed with Jeffrey. She hated him; at the same time she couldn't bear to lose him. She wanted to die, she was so embarrassed at being caught. She wanted to strangle Jeff because it was all his fault.

"Hello, Diana," he said coolly.

Diana paused, assessing the situation. Then she smiled charmingly at him. "Ah, Jeff, still the same old jock, I see. In town for a few weeks and you've already discovered afternoon delight.

Jeff didn't smile. "Diana, this is Jade McLane. Jade, Diana."

"How do you do?"

Diana moved into the room with no hesitancy, reaching out a hand to Jade. Jade automatically accepted the elegant hand, all the while furious at finding herself in such a situation. Diana, on the other hand, seemed amused and completely at ease. When her eyes fell on Jeff, they did so with possessive affection. She didn't seem to be at all alarmed or annoyed that she had discovered him with another woman.

Why should she be worried? Jade thought bitterly. *Look* at her. She knows that all she has to do to get Jeff back is to crook a finger.

"What are you doing here, Diana?" There was anger in Jeff's voice.

"Oh, don't be such a bear, Jeffrey. Jeff, Ms. McLane, I am sorry. I didn't mean to interrupt or barge in on anything. I just got to missing Ryan so terribly!"

"You could have called me."

"You know me, Jeff. I just hopped on a plane." Her voice faltered—very prettily, Jade thought. "Jeff, you've always promised that I could see him when I wanted. And you've always been so wonderful about it. I . . . I just didn't hesitate. You don't mind my coming to see my son?"

His jaw clenched; he closed his eyes a moment. "No, Diana, you know that you can always see Ryan."

Jade started looking for her shoes. She had to get out of the house and away from Jeffrey Martin.

Diana moved into the room and strolled over to the window. Jade wondered furiously if Jeffrey were imagining her naked there.

"This is a stunning place, Jeff," she said enthusiastically. "You *did* buy it? And Ms. McLane, you found it for him. I know, you see, because I went by your office. That nice man where Jeff is staying gave me the name of the firm. You must be very good. This place is perfect for Jeff."

"Yes, it's just perfect for him." Jade agreed stiffly, wanting only to leave as quickly as possible. She slid a foot into the shoe she found near the closet door.

Diana made a tsking sound and picked up Jeffrey's red plaid shirt. "Jeff, you're still as messy as ever. Always anxious..."

Jade found her other shoe. "Mrs. Martin, it was a pleasure meeting you," she said flatly. "Excuse me. I'm sure you two have a lot to discuss."

She fled from the room, barely aware of Jeff shouting her name. She didn't have her car, but it didn't matter. Her own house wasn't more than six or seven blocks away.

"Jade!"

He was chasing her down the stairway, still barefoot and shirtless. At the door he caught her arm. She went rigid, then strained desperately to escape him. She couldn't. His grip was like iron.

"What the hell's the matter with you?" he demanded furiously, and she wondered how his eyes had ever reminded her of the sky on a clear day. They looked like a dark tempest now.

"What's the matter with me?" she repeated in furious amazement. "How can you—"

"Dammit! I didn't invite her! She just barged in."

"Well, that's your problem, not mine!"

He swore and threw the door open. Maintaining his death grip on her arm, he dragged her down the driveway to his car.

"Let me go! I don't want to talk to you—"

"You damned well are going to talk to me. You can't go flying out on me like this. Not after this afternoon."

Again she tried to wrench her arm from his grasp. He only held her tighter. "Stop it!"

"I want you to let me go!" Tears stung her eyes suddenly, viciously. "Go back to your wife!"

"She's my ex-wife. Now you're going to listen to me whether you want to or not."

"I'm—"

He forced her into the car and slammed the door after her. Before she had a chance to get back out he was gunning the engine.

"You son of a bitch! You can't do this—"

"I believe I'm doing it."

The car screeched down the long drive, slid out onto the road and turned down Main onto Jade's street. They reached her driveway in record time.

Tears shimmered in Jade's eyes. "Damn you, Jeffrey Martin—"

He spun on her, taut as a wire, exasperated, frustrated, still furious—and a little bit desperate.

"No! Damn you, Jade! Damn you for thinking so little of us that you could possibly behave this way!"

He jerked the car door open and practically dragged her out. "Invite me in, Mrs. McLane, because I'm coming in whether you do or not. We are going to talk."

"I—"

"You, at the very least, are going to listen."

Chapter 8

Seconds later Jade was standing in her living room, amazed that he could be so angry with her when she was the one who had been wronged. But he was angry—terribly so. He paced the floor, casting her gazes that spoke of a wealth of emotion just barely held in control.

"What the hell is the matter with you? Running out like that! You weren't dragged into anything, you weren't coerced, and I was under the impression that you cared. Deeply. Yet all of a sudden you're hopping about like a teenager caught in the act by her parents. Damn it, Jade! I didn't ask her to come to Miami, but I can hardly forbid her to set foot in the city."

"Wait a minute! Wait just a minute! Your ex-wife crashes in on us and you're yelling at *me*?"

"I didn't go running out like a frightened rabbit!"

"And why would you have? You were the one she was there to see. You told me that you've slept with her since the divorce."

"I told you how long ago it was, too. And that we were never, never—in a thousand years never—going to get back together. Nice damned couple *we* make."

"Couple? Aren't you assuming a lot after just one afternoon?"

"Couple! And no I'm not assuming anything on that score. Hell, what is this? You sound as if you'd like to gift wrap me and hand me back to Diana. If you were ashamed of being in bed with me, maybe you shouldn't have been there at all."

"Maybe I shouldn't have been."

He chose to ignore that.

"And if you weren't ashamed, you shouldn't have run out as if you were."

He'd stopped pacing. He was staring straight at her. Challenging her, daring her—or pleading with her? She didn't know.

"If you mean so little to each other," Jade shouted, "why would she just waltz in on you like that?"

"Because we're not enemies!" Jeffrey shouted back. He raked his fingers through his hair and drew in a deep breath. "Jade, she missed Ryan. She came down, and Toby told her where to find me. I left the door open—I thought that I'd locked it."

Jade was silent for a second. She couldn't seem to think rationally. She had finally gone to bed with a man, a man she had been falling in love with, a man she had thought too perfect to be true. Idiot . . . well, she probably deserved this one. She'd known there was an ex-wife. What had she expected?

She'd expected Diana to stay in Chicago where she belonged.

"Dammit, Jade, do you care or not?"

Care? Yes, she cared. More than she wanted to admit. But she was frightened, too.

"I—"

"*What?*"

"Stop yelling at me! Yes! I care! That's why I'm frightened, you idiot! She's so beautiful, how can I compete? And you two are still so friendly. It unnerves me and it scares me and I don't know if I'm being an idiot—or intelligent enough to see what the outcome of all this might be."

He turned around and slammed a fist against the wall. "I won't let you do this," he said at last. "I just won't let you do it. You're everything I've been looking for, everything I've longed for, and dammit, we're perfect together. You *can't* say that it isn't so. Every day has been better than the one before, and you know it." He turned back and came to her, gripping her shoulders too tightly. "Jade. You can't just run out on me!"

She stared at him, swallowing, painfully aware that she hadn't wanted to run out on him. And she hadn't "run out"; she had run away—from Diana, from him and from herself. She'd been certain that she had lost the battle before it could even begin. But he had followed her. That had to mean something. Did it mean that he cared about her?

But if he knew that his marriage to Diana was over, he was alone in his conviction. Having met Diana, Jade was convinced that Jeffrey's ex-wife did not mean to maintain her "ex" status forever.

Jade was certain Diana didn't see her as a threat. Diana had been amused by the interlude, nothing more. Obviously, she was convinced that she would soon have a place in Jeffrey's life again. All she had to do was bide her time until he felt the irresitible pull of her beauty.

The worst part, Jade realized, was that she was terrified Diana might be right. Nonetheless, she was more in love with Jeffrey than ever. It hurt to be in love, but she cared about him so much that she was willing to gamble. She would pit herself against Diana, and pray that she was the one he would choose.

"Jeffrey..." She spoke his name in misery. He had told her that they were perfect together, that he wouldn't let her walk away. But what if it wasn't really true?

"Jade, I love you. Please, don't let her come between us."

She was in love. She had to believe him. She swallowed again. "Where is Diana now?"

"I don't know. I assume she's still at the house."

Jade closed her eyes, feeling a little ill.

"She's going to stay there?"

"Of course not!"

"But—"

"I didn't have time to talk to her. I had to sprint the five-hundred to catch up with you. All I told her was that she was always welcome to see her son, but that she'd caused a problem in my personal life and she'd just have to wait until I had talked to you."

"Is she...is she moving down here?"

"I have no idea."

"Oh, God..."

"Jade!" His arm slipped around her. He tilted her chin up with his free hand, forcing her eyes to meet his. "Didn't you *hear* me? Didn't you *listen*? Or doesn't it matter to you? I'm in love with you. I think it started the day we met. And the more I saw you, the more all the little things began to haunt me. The way you smiled. The way you looked. The sound of your voice. Your passion, your knowledge. I'd watch you pour water for the kids, and I couldn't remember where I was. I'd watch you talk to my son, laugh, ruffle his hair, and I was jealous of my own child. I wanted you to touch me so badly. The physical longing was constant agony—until this afternoon. But the other, the love, was always there, too, waiting to be nurtured. Jade, it's precious, and it's special, and some people never know it. You *can't* just throw it away because I was married before. I can't change that; even if I could, I probably wouldn't, because Ryan came from that marriage, and he has been the most wonderful part of my life. Jade!"

She was closing her eyes again. He'd said he loved her. She knew he probably wouldn't have said it today except that circumstances had pushed him.

"Jade . . ."

She opened her eyes.

"I love you, too, Jeff."

"Love me enough. Love me enough to stand by me."

She started to nod, but then she shook her head. "It's been such a short time since we met. I don't know what we are. I mean—"

"Lovers," he told her huskily.

"But only once."

His tension eased at last. The slow, easy, sensual smile that was so much a part of what she loved about him slid onto his mouth.

"I can change that."

"But Jeff—she's waiting. For you."

"She can wait."

It was insane. But didn't falling in love make a woman a little bit insane? His ex-wife had just interrupted them in bed, and now she was ready to crawl back into bed with him again.

"The kids..."

"Are fine. They're with Toby. We're alone. And we need time together for you to feel—"

"Feel secure?"

"For you to believe in me."

"I do believe in you."

She did. She believed when he kissed her, when sparklers of white light burst before her eyes and her body caught fire. It was just a kiss, but it made her body feel limp, and at the same time, it brought life to every pore, every cell, every nerve. She might have felt it even if he hadn't touched her. She might have known the same delicious ache if he'd just looked at her across the room. It was thrilling. It was the beautiful part of falling in love.

She found herself in his arms next. She was smiling into his eyes.

"I am crazy," she muttered.

"I love you," he told her. She reached up to touch his hair. She smoothed a lock behind his ear. He knew the way to her bedroom. In seconds they would lie down and tear at each other's clothing...

To her surprise, he didn't lie down on the bed. He went straight into the bathroom.

"Actually," she said, "you're crazy."

He laughed. "No, I'm not. I thought we could take a shower together. An intimate thing, hmm?"

She laughed, realizing that he was right. She needed, desperately wanted, all the intimate little moments with him. Because Diana had had them all.

Yet although they had known each other only a short time, it seemed as if they had been together forever. She felt no fear, no uneasiness with him. She was too enthralled by the sensation of his fingertips against her back as he unfastened the halter dress and let it fall to the floor. It was as if he had lived with her always. Quickly he adjusted the water, started the shower, shed his clothing and dragged her beneath the spray.

For a moment she felt the pulse of the water. Then he was behind her with the bar of soap. He slid his arms around her middle, soaping the undersides of her breasts, her belly and below. The coarse hair of his chest teased her back. The force of his desire thrilled her. His hands moved over her breasts, caressing them, teasing the nipples to peaks.

She gasped as he turned her, and shuddered with the delicious sensation of his body entering her. The water beat like the thunder of her pulse, heated her with his every thrust. Never had she known such excitement. Never had she known that movement could thrill her so easily.

She felt his hands on her hips, holding her, moving her, caressing her. Each touch intensified the excitement inside her. The feeling built and built, and she was dimly aware that her inarticulate cries joined with the rush and sizzle of the water.

She would have thought she'd hate making love in the shower, but it was sheer ecstasy. When the end finally came she could have fallen. He was there to catch her, to kiss her.

She stared up at him, her drenched hair flowing down her back, the lines of her face clean and beautiful. Her eyes were wide with awe.

"Can life really go on like this?" she wondered aloud.

He brought his hands to her face and cupped it. He kissed the tip of her nose, her forehead, her lips again.

"If you let it."

He turned off the water. They stepped from the shower and dried each other.

And then he brought her to the bed.

Finally, resting there in his arms, Jade voiced some of her fears.

"Jeffrey..."

"What?"

"I don't think you begin to see the problems we're going to face."

"I see them all."

"Ryan... Ryan is going to want..."

"Jade, naturally Ryan would like his mother and me to get back together. We've discussed it. I've told him that our life-styles are just too different."

A little boy is not going to understand that, Jade thought. But at the moment, she wasn't going to say so.

"Jade, I love you."

She sighed, still thrilled with her sense of physical well-being, but frightened, too.

"So you tell me, what happens now?"

"Now I'll go back and see Diana. I'll tell her to please knock when she appears at my house from now on. I'll explain that you are a permanent part of my life, one I'll never relinquish. Then I'll drive back to Toby's; she can take Ryan for the night, and tomorrow. I have to work tomorrow, anyway. I'll pick Sean up and bring him here. Unless you want to come with me."

"Come with you?"

"Sure."

Jade gnawed her lower lip slightly. She wanted to go with him, because she didn't want to let him out of her sight. But she didn't want to be a buffer between him and Diana. Someone to hold on to, just so that he didn't find himself in his ex-wife's arms.

No, he had to go alone. She wasn't even sure it would be right for him to come back tonight. For Ryan's sake, he should probably do something with Diana and his son.

"Jeff... no, I don't want to go with you. You and Diana have to straighten things out together." She swung around to stare at him. "I won't be a shield against her."

He laughed, holding her to him. "There's my ti-gress! But I don't need a shield against her.

"She's very beautiful."

"Yes, she is."

"You loved her once."

"Maybe. It was so long ago, I don't remember."

Jade was almost startled by his tone. He sounded bored by the thought of his ex-wife.

Oh, dear God, she prayed silently, please let that be true.

"I don't think you should get Sean. I'll get him. Why don't you take Diana and Ryan to dinner or—"

"No!" He was staring at her incredulously. "Jade, I won't play games like that."

"But Ryan—"

"I would do almost anything in the world for Ryan. I don't ever say anything derogatory about Diana to him. We make an effort to get along in front of him. But I won't—"

"Ryan will—"

"Jade, don't you see? It would be worse to do anything to encourage his fantasy that we could get back together."

"I think you're wrong."

"I'm not."

He stood up, stretched and headed for the bathroom to retrieve his clothing. Jade felt dizzy; her heart seemed to catch in her throat as she watched him. He was so beautiful in the nude. All muscled and without a speck of extra flesh. It made her tremble all over again just to see him and know that he had been hers.

He returned, dressed and bent to kiss her again. A shiver of misery struck her; he was going to see Diana.

"What's the matter?"

She shook her head. "Nothing. It's just—"

"Just what?"

"Just that I took so long to fall in love, and it's so painful. I was so slow, and so careful. I always knew that it would hurt. I thought I was mature and sophisticated and smart. And now this: I'm in love with a man who has a beautiful barracuda for an ex-wife and I know that disaster is looming ahead.''

She tried to laugh, but it didn't work. He sat down beside her and took her into his arms. ''Jade, I know it isn't going to be easy. I know that she's a problem, and that we'll have a few problems with Ryan. Please, Jade. Trust in me. Love me enough.''

''I want to,'' she whispered.

He kissed her lips. ''I'll be back soon.''

When he left, her imagination tormented her with visions of Diana smiling as he walked back into the house, of Jeffrey taking his ex-wife into his arms. Diana was just so beautiful. What man could resist her?

He would, he would, he would...

He had said that he loved her. She had to believe.

Despite her suggestion to the contrary, Jeff came back with Sean. Sean rattled away about the sleep-over, then he and Jeff went outside to throw a ball around while she prepared spaghetti and meatballs.

To a casual observer, it would have seemed like a pleasant evening, but to Jade, it was miserably tense. Jeff didn't mention Diana, and neither did Sean. When Jeff went home at ten, however, Jade decided to question her son. She walked to Sean's doorway and stood there, wondering if he was awake. He was, and she went in to sit down beside him.

''So the party was nice?''

''Oh, yeah, it was real nice. We had lots of fun.''

''Good. Was Ryan happy to see his mother?''

''Oh, yeah. And is she neat. A knockout!''

"A knockout?" Jade repeated. Sean wasn't particularly into girls yet—not unless they had extraordinary prowess with a baseball bat.

"That's what Toby called her. She really is neat. Almost as neat as Jeff."

Jade felt like chopped liver.

"Was Ryan upset that his father didn't go out to dinner with them?"

"I don't think so," Sean said, yawning. "He was too excited to see her."

He was falling asleep, so Jade kissed his cheek and left him.

The rest of her night was even more miserable than the first part. She hated herself for allowing Jeff to put her in such a position. It was pathetic to be so in love with a man, and not know whether she was really the woman he wanted.

I can't go on like this....

I can't give him up....

On Sunday, she knew that the movers were bringing Jeff's things to his house. She wondered if Diana was somehow supervising.

He called her Sunday night, saying that he expected Ryan back in about an hour. He told her that Diana had taken a room at one of the elegant hotels by the Mayfair in the Grove.

Jade was happy to know that Diana was definitely not staying at Jeff's house. But she was miserable when she thought about Diana seeing Jeff again in an hour.

She barely slept that night. The next morning, she had to drag herself into the office.

Jeff came by at eleven and asked her to lunch. Sandy cheerfully told her to go and to take her time.

"Where shall we go?" Jeff asked her when they were sitting in the Lincoln. She stared at him and thought that he looked wonderful in his beautifully tailored suit. She wanted to reach out and touch his clean-shaven cheeks. Just looking at him brought back vivid memories of the day before. She heard the echo of her whimpers when he'd made love to her, felt the trembling warmth inside her, the excitement, the fever. . . .

She looked away, hating herself a little bit for being so weak where he was concerned.

"I—"

"What?"

She turned to him again, feeling unreasonably sad and wistful. "I don't want lunch. I want to go to your house."

Fire leaped to his eyes; his knuckles grazed her cheek tenderly.

He gunned the Lincoln as if it were a sports car, and they sped down the road.

She was glad of what she had said. They laughed like guilty children, racing into the house, strewing clothing everywhere and making love. Afterward, they found wine and cheese in the refrigerator and took it back to the bedroom, where they ate and then made love again. Jade didn't mention Diana; she didn't want the other woman to be a part of her time with Jeff.

He didn't mention her, either, and Jade didn't feel the doubts again until that night, when she lay in her own bed, alone.

* * *

At the baseball field the next day, Jade sat beside Lynn and Miriam Hodges while the kids caught balls out in the field. Jade had always been close to Lynn; she wasn't really accustomed to baring her soul to Mariam Hodges, but Miriam had been picking up Timmy at Toby's house when Diana had appeared with Jeff.

"I don't know what on earth you're worried about," Lynn was saying. "From what I understand, that is one affair that is really over."

Jade chewed idly on a piece of grass, shrugging. "Get serious, Lynn. Have you ever seen anyone as beautiful as Diana?"

"You're not exactly ugly."

Miriam sniffed dramatically. "Lynn! Certainly, Jade is pretty, but come on—it's like pitting the Ivory Girl against Bo Derek."

"Thanks a lot," Jade grumbled, staring out at the field.

"Are you in love with him?" Miriam demanded.

"What's love?" Jade returned blithely.

Lynn laughed. "I remember falling in love. It was the greatest thing in the world. First you see someone, and you're attracted. And it's as if you sizzle inside every time you see him again. Then it's lots of little things: the way he combs his hair, his grin, the way his fingers look when they touch your arm, his scent—"

"And when you're not in love," Miriam interrupted, "all those same things become a horror. You don't remember his cologne, but how awful he smells when he sweats."

"Miriam!" Lynn flashed her a glance of annoyance.

"Well, it's true," Miriam persisted stubbornly. "There was this guy I dated for a while. He was gorgeous. I thought I might be falling in love, and then I knew that I wasn't. He loved anchovies and I hated the smell of them on his breath. He combed his hair for an hour three times a day. The initial attraction had been there, but not the love. He might have been good-looking, but he was affected, too. In the end, I wondered what I was doing with him. Real love is when those little things—endearing or not so endearing—are all special and tolerable because underneath, being together is far more important than anything else."

"I can't imagine Jeff Martin having any not so endearing qualities," Lynn said.

But he does, Jade thought. He has an ex-wife who would scare off braver women than I.

"I definitely think you should keep dating him," Miriam told her.

"Oh. Why is that?" Jade queried, smiling dryly. "You've just told me I'm going to lose him."

"Oh, don't be huffy, Jade," Miriam said, an elegant hand waving in the air. "I didn't say that at all. But even if you do, look at all the good the man has done you already."

"What do you mean?"

"He had your car fixed, didn't he? And look at the monstrous commission you made on the sale of that house. Honey, he's *loaded*."

"Miriam!" Lynn and Jade protested together.

Miriam ignored them. "Oh, that's not all, of course. He's sexy. Macho. Tender. Clint Eastwood minus fifteen years and a Magnum. But besides that, Jade, you could do all right with him, win or lose.''

Jade narrowed her eyes. ''Miriam, just what are you saying?''

''Don't go flying off the handle. Just think what you could get out of him.''

''You think I should see him for his money?'' Jade demanded.

''Oh, not for his money,'' Miriam giggled. ''I think you should see him for sexual fulfillment. I would. I'd love to. What's he like, by the way? The best thing since the hoola-hoop, I'll bet.''

''Miriam!''

''See him for his face, his body, his wink, his smile, his dimples and that great voice. Money is just a side benefit that you could keep in mind. Men love to shower their lovers with gifts; you've already gotten a few.''

Jade suddenly felt a little queasy. Miriam wasn't trying to hurt her—she was just being Miriam.

Neither Jade nor Lynn had a chance to reply. Toby's long legs suddenly appeared before them.

''What is this? A hen party? You cats baring your claws again?''

''We weren't discussing you, dear,'' Lynn said sweetly.

''Hmm. Well, up then! I need a scorekeeper. We've got a practice game with the Pitacci Pizzas in about sixty seconds. Our guys are on the bench first. Hup, hup, ladies—let's get moving!''

They all scrambled to their feet. Lynn picked up the score sheets and clipboard; Jade started dispensing paper cups of water to the sweaty little boys lined up on the bench. Jeff was giving them a pep talk.

"Okay, we all know that Killer Callahan is pitching first for them. And we all know that he's a little wild. Just stand your ground, and if it's no good, guys, don't hit at it. Take the walk. We can beat him, right?"

"Right!"

"Okay, let's play ball!"

Seconds later, Jeff was standing by to coach at first base. Jade was assigned to keep the kids in batting order. Two of their team went up and struck out. Sean was third up to bat. Jade rooted for him along with the rest of the team, and she couldn't help smiling when he knocked the ball halfway out of the park and made a home run.

All the while, she had a problem: her eyes wouldn't stay away from Jeff. Tanned and trim, looking boyish in jersey and shorts, he watched Sean slide in to home plate.

"Oh, Ryan, you're up!" she exclaimed, tearing her eyes away from his father.

She handed him a bat, and he stepped up to the plate. Killer Callahan sent out two wild pitches. Ryan held his bat steady. She saw him glance at his father, and saw Jeff give him a nod that indicated he was doing darned well.

But then Killer Callahan wound up for another pitch. This time, Ryan couldn't sidestep the ball. It hit his thigh with a sickening sound. Ryan screamed and fell down.

Don't run immediately, don't run immediately.... Lynn had always warned her not to make too big a thing of little injuries.

But she had heard the sound of the ball; she had heard the sound of Ryan's cry.

Jeff was far away. She was right there behind the fence.

"Don't—" Lynn began behind her, but then Ryan screamed again.

"Go," Lynn told her.

She didn't need the command. She was already racing around the fence. When she reached Ryan, she fell on her knees, her heart pounding in a fury as she put an arm around his quivering shoulders.

Chapter 9

Toby was already there, standing over Ryan. Jeff was running in from the field. All that Jade saw was Ryan.

Something special happened between the two of them. Ryan looked into her eyes and slipped his arms around her shoulders, burying his face against her neck. She held him while Toby asked the questions.

"It hit your thigh?"

Ryan nodded against her. Someone was saying that the pitch had been frightfully hard; someone else mumbled that his leg could be broken. By then Toby was carefully probing Ryan's thigh, and assuring everyone that it wasn't broken.

"You're going to have a bruise, a heck of a bruise, buddy," Toby told him.

"Let's get some ice, huh, Ryan?" Jade said. He nodded, still keeping his face against her shoulder. He was nine years old, and nine-year-olds tried very hard not to cry. But almost every kid there had been hit by a stray pitch somewhere along the line, and there wasn't one of them who was going to give a wounded teammate anything but sympathy. Jade knew it, but she wasn't sure if Ryan did. "Come on, lean on me."

A hand fell on her shoulder as she struggled to rise. "I've got him. I'll take care of him," she said.

"He, uh, is my son, you know," Jeff said easily from behind her. His eyes met hers with a tenderness and understanding that warmed her all over.

"You okay, son?" Jeff asked Ryan, picking him up and carrying him off the field with Jade following. Lynn and Miriam ran up, and Jade went to the cooler to make an ice pack.

When she returned, Jeffrey had put Ryan down on the ground and was checking the rising lump on his thigh. "It's going to be black and blue for weeks. How are you doing?"

"Okay," Ryan said. His tears had dried; he was looking at his father for assurance, and Jeff was giving him just that.

"Toby told me that last year Killer Callahan hit every kid on the team. He must have known he missed you and had to get one in."

Jade knelt down silently, and put the ice pack on Ryan's leg. "You'd better go back to the game, Dad," Ryan told him.

"You'll be okay?"

"Jade is with me. Go back, Dad."

"Yeah, Jade is with you. I guess I'll go back," Jeff said. He winked at Ryan, then left his son and Jade together.

Jade looked up just in time to see the little boy's eyes following his father. Then he sighed.

"Does it still hurt?" Jade asked him.

"Just a little."

"It will last awhile, but it won't be that bad," Jade said. She smiled. "Callahan got Sean on the thumb last year. Sean lost the nail."

"I'll bet he didn't cry," Ryan said wistfully.

Jade laughed. "Wrong. He bellowed like a bull."

Ryan laughed, and she saw the same warmth in the child's eyes as she did in the father's. Oh, you Martins! she thought. Both blue-eyed heartbreakers!

But then he looked away from her. "Sean is so good, though. I should be good—my father was great."

Jade hesitated just a second. "Ryan, people have different interests. You know your dad is going to be proud of anything that you choose to do. You don't have to play baseball because of him."

"Oh, but I want to play. I really do! I just wish that I were better at it."

"Well, then you keep working at it, and you will be," Jade promised.

"I will!" Ryan said enthusiastically. "I will." He flushed a little. "Do you think the ice has been on long enough?"

Jade lowered her eyes. Ryan had just become aware that his underwear was showing.

"Sure."

She moved the pack from his thigh, dumped the ice, and wrung out the towel. She scrambled to her feet and offered him a hand. He took it. When he stood, he slipped an arm around her for balance. She felt very close to him as she helped him slowly limp back to the field.

The game was just ending. The boys were all cheering and throwing their caps in the air—Toby's team had taken the game. Every one of them came running up to see how Ryan was doing; they were all shouting their own war stories about being hit at various times. Ryan flushed with pleasure at the attention. He still held tightly to Jade until his father appeared, and then he went happily into Jeffrey's arms.

"How're you doing, sport?" Toby asked him, flipping his cap over his eyes. "Not afraid now, are you?"

"No, sir," Ryan said.

Jade, who had been watching Ryan, suddenly realized that Jeff was looking at her with approval and something more. She didn't quite understand the look in his eyes; she only knew that she basked in it, as eager as Ryan for his approval.

"Hey! A Maserati!" one of the kids called out, suddenly.

Jade didn't understand the significance of those words at first. She didn't think anything of them. But suddenly Ryan was stiffening in his father's arms.

"Mom!" he called out joyously, wiggling to escape his father's hold. Jade stared at the street where Diana was just stepping out of a parked Maserati. Ryan—barely limping at all in his eagerness—was already racing toward her.

"Damn her," Jeffrey breathed.

Jade looked at him quickly. His features were tense with anger and exasperation.

Jade felt sick. "Why?" she said suddenly, angrily. "Why, if your relationship is really over, is she always where you are?"

"What do you expect me to do?" he asked angrily. "Tell her she can't come to practice, can't see her son? I'd alienate him completely. And I told you—I've no right to keep her out of the state."

Everyone had drifted off the field by then, and Jeffrey stalked off after Ryan. Jade clenched her teeth and followed.

All the boys were hovering around Ryan and Diana, and Jade quickly discovered why. Diana had invited all the kids out for ice cream and had included their parents in the invitation, too. She laughed and spoke easily with Toby, Lynn and Miriam. Then she saw Jade.

"Ms. McLane, how nice to see you again. You'll come, won't you, you and Sean? For ice cream? After all, the team just won its first game."

Once again, Diana looked like a fashion plate. She wore a form-hugging red knit dress, and her pitch-black hair fanned out sleekly over her shoulders. The whole pack of little nine-year-olds seemed as infatuated with her as their fathers.

"I don't think so, thank you," Jade said.

"Mom!" Sean whispered miserably, pulling her hand. She couldn't blame him. It appeared that all the other kids were going.

"I've had a long day, Sean—" she began, but Jeffrey was suddenly behind her, his hands tight on her shoulders.

"Let him go. I'll bring him home."

He wasn't going to try to convince her to go with them. Jade wasn't sure if she was resentful or glad.

"All right," she said.

"Dad!" Ryan called out. "I'll ride with Mom!"

"Sure. You should thank Jade, though."

Ryan looked at Jade, and the gaze he gave her was startling in its resentment. It was so different from the way he had looked at her before. The bond was gone, gone completely. She might have been the Wicked Witch of the West.

"Thank you," he said stiffly, and then he disappeared into his mother's Maserati.

"I'll wring his neck," Jeff muttered.

"No." Jade spun around. "You won't say a word to him. Jeffrey, I mean it."

He shrugged; she didn't know if she had won her point or not. "Sean, let's go." He gazed at Jade grimly. "We'll be back soon."

While everyone else went for ice cream Jade went home and poured herself a huge glass of wine. She took a shower and then poured herself another huge glass of wine and paced the living room floor.

By the time Jeff reached the house, Jade was in no mood to see him. He had left Ryan in the car, so he gave her a quick kiss and turned to leave as soon as Sean had run into his bedroom. "I'll call you," he said.

"Don't bother. Not until you've got your past straightened out."

"Jade, do you know what you sound like?" he asked, coming back in. "What the hell am I supposed to do?"

"I don't know what you're supposed to do," she retorted. "Something."

"You're doing exactly what she wants."

"I don't know what I'm doing—I just can't stand this!"

"Jade—" He tried to take her into his arms; she spun away from him.

"I mean it! Straighten your life out first—then call me."

For just a second, he looked violent. His eyes were dark as ink, his jaw tense, his entire form taut as wire.

He threw his hands into the air. "Fine."

Then he walked out of the house. Jade watched him go and burst into tears. She sat down on the sofa and didn't even notice that Sean had walked back into the room until he put an arm around her. She tried to dry her tears, but her son knew her well.

"Mom, he doesn't even like her."

She caught his hand and smiled through her tears. "I'm sorry, Sean, I—"

"You're not being fair, Mom. What's he supposed to do?"

"Sean—"

He interrupted her with a vast sigh. "I know—it's none of my business and I'm going to bed."

She laughed. "No—it is your business, in a way. I love you. I just can't . . . Oh, never mind. I can't explain. Let's both go to bed, huh?"

Her words were cheerful enough. But she didn't think she fooled her son, and she certainly didn't fool herself.

She spent the night wide awake, pounding her pillow and feeling sorry for herself. At 1:00 a.m., she decided she had been unfair. At 2:00 a.m., she was wondering what else she could have done. At four she slept from sheer exhaustion. At six-thirty, the alarm went off, and she knew she was in for a miserable day.

At seven, right before she went in to wake Sean up, the phone started ringing. She hesitated, not knowing if she dreaded hearing Jeff's voice or longed for it.

When she answered, he didn't wait for anything more than her initial "Hello" before starting in.

"I want to see you. As soon as possible. Lunch?"

His voice brought all sorts of things back to her. An awful ache of longing, as if it had been weeks instead of hours since she had seen him. She could close her eyes and see his smile, the way the short dark hairs curled on his chest, the darkness of his fingers when they rested against her flesh, the way his eyes looked when they were filled with passion. She could hear his voice, whispering words of love and encouragement.

"Jade—"

"Jeff, maybe you should give it a go with Diana. For your son's sake. Maybe—"

He interrupted her with a string of violent oaths. "Come on, Jade . . . be serious! Do you know how foolish that sounds? If it were necessary, I'd happily lie down and die for Ryan. But pretending that Diana and I could ever make it would only hurt him. Surely you realize that! Jade—"

"I don't know!" she wailed. "I just don't know!"

"Lunch—"

"No . . . no! Not today!"

She slammed the phone back on to the hook, then removed it. If he tried to call back, he'd get a busy signal.

He didn't call her at work, and her phone didn't ring once that night.

Nor did it ring Wednesday morning. And on Wednesday night, the only calls she received were from Lynn and Miriam. Neither mentioned Jeff—or Diana.

Thursday afternoon, she didn't go to practice. She asked Miriam to take both boys.

She made it through Friday and the weekend. But she didn't sleep well, and Sandy actually snapped at her, calling her a zombie.

On Monday morning, she found herself sipping tea and staring at the phone at 6:00 a.m. She was furious with herself, because she was just waiting for the clock to slip around to seven so that she could call him.

When he answered, she went tense all over.

"Have you any time today?" she asked, her voice cool.

He answered slowly, as stiff as she.

"Yes, when?"

"Eleven, eleven-thirty?"

"Yes. Where?"

Jade drew in a deep breath. "I'll come by your house."

He was silent for several seconds, then he laughed a little bitterly. "I'm supposed to be after your body, Ms. McLane, not the other way around."

"Forget it—" she began.

"I'll be here all morning. Just come by whenever you feel like it."

He hung up on her. She thought about calling him back, then she thought about just not showing up.

But at eleven o'clock she left her office and drove to the Grange. The gates were open. And the door opened, too, before she could bring her hand up to knock.

What was she going to say to him? she wondered as the door drifted inward, her hand still in the air.

Then he was there, towering over her slightly. He closed the door decisively behind her.

Words, words, words—where were the right words?

But she didn't need them. As soon as the door closed, his arms were around her. His lips touched hers in an explosion of heat and urgency. She was so stunned at first that she did not respond; his teeth tugged impatiently at her lower lip. Her lips parted, and fireworks went off as his tongue penetrated deep into her mouth. She was filled with a sense of urgency, a feeling that she would die if she did not have all of him quickly.

His lips left hers to rain kisses on her face. Sunlight streamed through the house, hit the windows, reflected in a dazzle of gold. But that light did not burn as brightly as the liquid gold that filled her.

"I missed you so badly," he whispered. His hands were at the neckline of her blouse. She felt his scent wash over her. Her palm came to his cheek.

"I had to come."

"I couldn't have waited for you much longer."

They were standing in the beautiful foyer with the marble floor, encircled by windows, but she paid no heed to their surroundings. She found her hands on him, her fingers trembling in their hurry to divest him of his shirt.

"Jade..."

"I can't help it. I love you."

"I love you."

Her silk blouse fell to the marble with a whisper. His fingers were on her bra hook and then on the bare flesh of her back. He inhaled raggedly as he caressed her breasts, crushing her against his bare chest. She shivered at the touch of his naked chest against hers, the coarse hair erotic against her nipples.

"I missed you. Missed you—"

"So badly."

"All I've thought about—"

"I haven't slept."

"I've wanted you. Nothing else."

Their shoes were off. Her stockings and his socks followed. Her skirt joined her blouse in a soft heap. The marble was cold against their feet; maybe it wasn't so cold, maybe it was just that they were so very hot.

"I love you." He said it vehemently, harshly. "I love you, I love you, I love you."

She was in his arms, and they were moving up the stairs. There were so many windows, all of them open to the sun, and they were naked beneath it. Jade didn't feel at all exposed. Beyond the windows were two acres of lush foliage, like a jungle, stretches of banyan and seagrape as wild as any primeval land.

Moments later she was on his bed, feeling the cool sheets, the heat of his body. She loved him with every fiber of her being. She drank him in as if it had been a lifetime since she had seen him. She noticed all the little things she loved: the arch of his brow, the line of his mouth, the texture of his cheek, his chest, his hip. . . his manhood. Everything. She was starved for him. She needed the feel of his fingers stroking her, the caress of his mouth, his kiss, the pressure of his body.

"Yes. . ."

"Oh, yes..."

Time stood still. They made love in a frenzy, then they made love all over again, slowly; once again, they came together in a frenzy. Her energy could not be depleted; each time she tired, he aroused her again. Each time she thought herself entirely sated, she learned that he could touch her in a new erogenous zone, and her desire would come bursting to life again.

Eventually, she took a sheet from the bed, wrapped it around herself and sat before the tower window, looking out at the water. She knew he was watching her from the bed. She knew that he was feeling lazy and contented, yet his eyes were sharp, as if he wanted to read her words in her face before she spoke them.

"What's the matter?"

"I don't know. When I'm with you, everything is perfect. When I have to leave, the anxiety sets in again. The fear, the wondering."

"You have to believe that I love you."

She smiled softly, ruefully. "I do. I can't help it. It's just that I know all the other parents in the league are talking about us. I know that your ex-wife is watching us with amusement. I know that everyone assumes I'm a brief fling for you—after all, you are Jeffrey Martin. I'm a passing fancy, an ordinary person. I know people think I should just enjoy it while it lasts. After all, I'm deriving such benefits from our relationship. My car, the commission on this place. Hell, according to some of them, I should hang in until I wind up with a pair of diamond earrings or something."

He was smiling, she noted, smiling very lazily, with all the charm that had captured her in the first place.

She stood up, clutching the sheet around her, approaching him angrily.

"You find that amusing?"

She threw a pillow on top of him. He laughed and asked her. "Would you like a pair of diamond earrings?

"No."

"You didn't mind the commission from the house."

"I'm a real estate agent. That's what I do for a living. I earned that."

"I'd say you've earned a dozen pairs of diamond earrings, too."

"You son of a bit—"

She raised a hand to hit him; he caught it and then laughed as he pulled her beneath him.

"Jade! I'm teasing! I can't see why you let the opinions of others bother you. You were the one after my body today, remember?"

"I wasn't—"

"You were. As desperately as I was after yours."

"So?"

He smiled again, a crooked, sensual grin. He laughed softly, and planted a light kiss on her lips.

"So marry me."

"What?"

"Marry me. That is what people do when they're in love, isn't it? Marry me—shut them all up."

She didn't answer right away. It was so sudden. She had been so afraid that he wanted to marry Diana again that Jade had never even thought about his proposing to her.

"Well?"

"I—"

"You claim to love me."

"I do. I just—"

"What?"

"I don't know." She closed her eyes.

"Maybe I'm afraid that marrying you would make me . . . what they say. A gold digger."

He groaned. "Can't we forget the damned money? This is ridiculous."

"We can't just get married."

"Why not?"

"Because. Ryan will have a fit—"

"Ryan will come around."

"He wants you to get back together with his mother—"

"Which will never happen. There's no point in allowing him to live under that delusion."

"Then there's Diana."

"What about her?" His eyes narrowed.

"I don't want to be a buffer—"

"A buffer? Damn you, Jade. You claim to love me, yet you don't trust a thing I say."

"Jeff! She is the most beautiful woman I've ever seen. How—"

"She's beautiful, Jade, yes. A painting can be beautiful, and a dress can be beautiful. A house, a day, a sunset. All in different ways. A child can be beautiful. An old woman handing cookies to a little girl can be beautiful. Real beauty is in the heart, Jade. Diana is beautiful to look at, but she is entirely self-centered. I tried to make it work for Ryan's sake. I tried a long, long time before I filed for divorce. But I realized that sacrificing my own happiness did not make me a good parent. You can't be miserable and make life good for others at the same time. I don't hate Diana. But any love I felt for her died a long time before we parted.''

"But you—''

"Yes, after we divorced, I was with her a few times. It didn't mean anything, except that adults have needs. She holds no lure for me that I can't resist. I hope she lives long, well, happily and merrily—just so long as it isn't with me. Jade, I am in love with you. I'm in love with everything that we can have together. A lifetime of loving, of waking up together, going to sleep together. Coming home every night of our lives to be together. Believing in each other. Even arguing—together. Meals together. A life together. Honest-to-God together. Jade, I want that. I want that more than I could ever tell you in words. Yes, it will be hard. Yes, Ryan is going to be a problem. Yes, I'm going to have to ask you to tolerate some difficult moments. And in return, I can only swear that I love you. Really love you. With all my heart, all of me.''

She stared into his eyes and was mesmerized by the love she saw there.

"Yes,'' she whispered.

"Yes?''

"I'll marry you.''

He held her cheeks between his palms, and kissed her lips lightly, with reverence. Then he kissed her with a newfound hunger. Finally he lifted his lips from hers.

"You are beautiful,'' he told her. "Outside, inside. I've never known anyone as beautiful as you. When we make love and I see the emotion, the passion and the caring in your eyes, you're beautiful. Honest and real and beautiful. And to my eyes, no other woman can compare."

"Oh, Jeffrey," she said, and tears stung her eyes. "When?"

"When?"

"When can we get married?"

He paused just a second. Then he grinned. "Next week. Sunday, as soon as I'm off work, we'll fly to Georgia. Monday we'll be married. We could get a license here and be married in three days, but I'd rather go away. I'd like to have a little time together—alone."

"The boys—"

"Toby and Lynn will happily take the kids for a few days. I wish it could be more, but we both have so many commitments right now. How does it all sound to you?"

She just nodded, a little dazed.

"What about my work?"

"That's up to you. Keep your job if you want; chuck it if you don't. Just do me one more favor."

"What's that?"

"Be late getting back from lunch today. Make love with me one more time . . . give me a few dreams so I can survive this last week of waiting."

"Oh, yes," Jade breathed. "Oh, yes . . ."

Chapter 10

Jade and Jeff decided not to say anything to the boys until Friday. Then the four of them could have dinner together somewhere, go to a movie or for a walk, and the two adults could break the news to the boys.

Sean, she was certain, would be ecstatic.

Ryan, she was equally certain, would be upset.

But she had stopped mentioning that fact; every time she did, Jeff scowled and said he was sorry, but Ryan would just have to be upset.

Jade had to agree that Jeff couldn't live his life to humor Ryan. In the end, such a thing would actually be cruel to the child. Still, news of his father's marriage was going to hit Ryan hard.

When Jade and Sean arrived at the Grange the next day, they were in for a surprise. The front door was opened by an elderly woman who looked perfect for the role of somebody's grandmother. She had snow white hair pulled back into a bun, dark merry eyes, red cheeks and a spotless white apron over a plump little body.

"Hello?" she inquired cheerfully.

"Uh, hi," Jade said. "I'm Jade Mc—"

"Oh, yes! Come in, dear, come in! And this must be Sean!"

Sean gave Jade a quizzical gaze that silently asked, Oh, no! She isn't going to kiss me, is she?

The woman laughed delightedly. "I'm Mattie Percival. I worked on and off for Jeff in Chicago—he had a much smaller place there, though. I'm going to be his full-time housekeeper here." She glanced at Sean with a winning smile. "Ryan is out back, playing. Why don't you go join him? I'll throw some hot dogs and hamburgers on the grill for you two in a few minutes, if you'd like."

Sean nodded, relieved that he wasn't going to be kissed. He glanced at Jade for permission, and she inclined her head. Sean mumbled out a "Thanks" to Mattie Percival, then went racing out.

Mattie looked at Jade, openly surveying her and seeming to approve of what she saw. "Thought I'd get the young man out of the way for a minute, since I understand the boys haven't been told the good news yet. I want to rephrase what I said. I'm the full-time housekeeper—with your approval."

Jade laughed. "You definitely have my approval, and it's nice to know it counts. Is Jeff here?"

"He certainly is. He's upstairs in his den. Go right on up."

"Thanks," Jade replied. She started up the stairs, then paused, smiling back at Mattie a little uncertainly. A housekeeper. Full-time. It was a nice thought. "Mattie?"

"Yes?"

"Would you mind terribly—I've put in a long day at the office and I'd love a drink."

"I have some chilled Chablis. I'll be right up with some frosted glasses."

Jade hurried on up the stairway. The doorway to the den was open; Jeff was sitting at the desk, poring over a set of newspaper clippings. He probably was planning his next telecast. She paused, wondering if she should interrupt his work.

"Jeff?"

He glanced up at her, and his slow, easy, wonderfully crooked grin wiped away all her doubts about disturbing him. He stood, coming to her quickly and taking her into his arms for a quick but breathtaking kiss.

"I didn't know you were coming," he said to her, still holding her and staring into her eyes as if he could never see enough of her face. "I would have warned you about Mattie. What do you think? This place is so big. She's going to have some extra help now and then for floors and things, but she's crazy about kids, and she's a miracle worker when it comes to keeping order."

"I think she's wonderful," Jade said.

"Great."

"I—"

A shriek—a loud, loud shriek—suddenly made its way up the stairs. Then another, even louder. Their eyes widened with alarm. Together, they turned and raced down the stairs.

Mattie, flushed and alarmed, was running into the living room, wringing her hands in her apron.

"Jeff! I don't know what got *into* them. I can't stop them. The boys—all of a sudden—"

Jeff rushed on past Mattie, out the door to the backyard. Jade was hot on his heels. She gasped when she got outside, astounded to see Sean and Ryan rolling on the ground in an intense and bitter struggle. Sean was on top, with a fistful of Ryan's hair clutched in his fingers.

Jeff lost no time in pulling Sean away from Ryan, his face a hard mask as he separated the two boys. He kept them at arm's length as he asked harshly, "What in God's name is this all about?"

Both boys were stubbornly silent. Jade swallowed, painfully aware that Ryan was going to have a shiner, while Sean's lip was swollen and bloody.

"What is going on here?" Jeff demanded again in a voice that brooked no disobedience.

"You tell him!" Sean raged at Ryan. Tears filled his eyes. "You tell him what you said!"

"It's true!" Ryan shrieked back, fighting his father's hold.

"*What?*" Jeff's voice boomed.

Ryan suddenly looked a little white, a little frightened and very small. But he straightened his spine, clenched his jaw so that it looked very similar to his father's and spoke.

"His mother!" He pointed at Sean. "His mother is nothing but a tramp and a whore and she's only after your money and your position."

Jade gasped from the doorway, stunned not only by Ryan's language, but by the venom in his voice.

After her gasp there was a miserable silence. Utter silence, in which only the breeze whispering through the trees could be heard.

That silence made the sound of Jeffrey's palm striking Ryan's behind all the worse.

"No," Jade breathed. "Jeff, no..."

But it was too late. Ryan was already pulling away from his father and racing toward the house. He turned back to stare at Jeff, tears streaming down his face. "It's true, it's true, it's true! You can beat me forever, and it will still be true!" he screamed.

He turned again, ignoring Jade's outstretched hand as he tore into the house.

Then Sean burst into tears, too. Jeff put a hand on his shoulder; Sean shook it off.

Jeff took an angry step toward the house, but Jade caught his sleeve, stopping him.

"Let me go. He can't go around talking like that. He's going to apologize, and he's going to do it now."

"No!" Jade moistened her lips to speak, shaking her head vehemently. "Don't. We both know he didn't think that up by himself. He's just repeating what he's been told."

She didn't think she'd ever seen Jeff look so hard or so cold, and for a moment she shivered inside, glad that his anger was not directed at her. "Jeff, listen to me, please! Just let it go."

"Let it go! I'll be damned if I will! He needs to learn a lesson, and Diana needs to learn one, too! She's the one who's filled his head with such garbage. By God, I'll kill her! I'll wring her neck. I'll—"

"No! Dammit, Jeff! This time, just let it all go. Don't you see—Diana wants a reaction, and that's exactly what you're giving her. Jeff, please...."

"She can't keep poisoning Ryan like this!"

"Jeff—"

"All right! All right!"

He stormed back into the house, past Mattie, into the kitchen. Jade went over to Sean, slipped an arm around his shoulders and hugged him close. She could hear Jeff even though the kitchen was some distance away. He was pouring himself a drink.

"Let's go home for now, huh?" Jade whispered to Sean.

"Forever!" Sean said violently. There were still tears in his eyes. "I hate Ryan! I hate him!"

"No, no, don't say that, Sean," she said softly. "He really doesn't mean to hurt me. He's just hurt inside himself. Can you understand that?"

Sean shook his head violently. Jade sighed. She bade Mattie a quiet goodbye and turned to leave. She wasn't going to talk to Jeff again in his present mood.

He was at her office in the morning before she was, talking to Sandy. Jade greeted him with a curious, worried look and was further perplexed when he refused to let her sit behind her desk.

"We're going," he told her.

"Where?"

"To Georgia."

"But—"

"Sandy's got everything under control here in the office. We'll be back by seven tonight. Toby is picking up Sean from school; Mattie will get Ryan."

"But—"

"We're going to get married this morning. I've got a car waiting for us at the Atlanta airport. We'll get the license, see a justice and have the afternoon together. We've got a flight back out at five-thirty, which brings us home at seven."

"But—" Jade tried again.

"Get out of here," Sandy interrupted this time. "You'll miss your flight out."

Jade was still uneasy, still trying to argue, as their plane lifted high above Miami and a smiling stewardess slipped a complimentary glass of champagne into her hand.

"This is too sudden! After last night—"

"I know it's sudden," Jeff put in impatiently. "Look, I'm sorry," he said tenderly, picking up her hand and playing with it idly. "I'd meant for us to have some time together, some special time alone. But I guess it's going to have to come later. I really wanted the works for a honeymoon, something wonderful. Paris, Hawaii. Long, lazy days just to be together." He smiled ruefully. "I wanted to make you deliriously happy. I'm sorry it isn't working out the way I'd hoped."

"I don't care about a honeymoon," she said mechanically. "Or Paris, or Hawaii, or any place or thing like that. But Jeff, I was thinking that maybe we should wait. Maybe we should let Ryan get accustomed to the idea of our marriage. We might really cause him some psychological harm—"

Jeff's fingers tightened around hers, and his face hardened into the determined look she had seen the night before. "We're going to do it, and he's going to learn to live with it."

"But, Jeff, Sean and Ryan hate each other now. They used to be best friends—"

"And they will be again."

"I have no right to do this without telling Sean."

"He'll understand."

"Jeff—"

He released her fingers impatiently. "I'm not going to beg, Jade. I'm in love with you. I can't stand living in separate houses anymore. Why should we have to snatch moments alone like two guilty high school seniors? I want to be married, man and wife, living together, sleeping together, sharing a room, with no excuses or pretense. I can't go on this way. And it isn't doing the kids any good, either. I love my son. I would do just about anything in the world for him—except let him grow up to be a little brat because of his mother's mind games. If I'm asking too much of you, fine. We'll go to Atlanta, look around and have lunch and come home. We'll forget the whole marriage bit. Then we can stop seeing each other. That will make Ryan happy—and Diana. Is that what you want?"

"It sounds like a threat," Jade retorted.

Jeff shook his head impatiently. "Maybe it is. I don't know. I just know that I don't want to tiptoe around. I love you; I need you." For all his protestations of love, his tone was as cold as ice. He glanced at his watch. "We still have an hour in the air; you've got an hour to decide what you want."

She felt like crying. It was a threat: Marry me now, or never see me again. She wanted to dump her champagne over his head; she wanted to tell him that he wasn't being fair, that they needed time to work out their problems.

But she didn't speak to him. She stared straight ahead and blinked back tears. God. She was a coward. She was afraid of Diana—afraid of Ryan, even.

What if Jeff was using her as a buffer? Legally married to Jade, he couldn't easily remarry his ex-wife. He'd have a woman at home, a preventative against finding himself in bed again with the wicked beauty who had once hurt him so badly, yet was so lovely that he feared he could not resist her.

Tears welled up in her eyes again; stubbornly, she refused to let them fall. She still didn't look at Jeff, but she could sense him beside her, smell the masculine fragrance of his after-shave, feel the vitality of his movement, the heat of his body. She was even aware of the texture of his suit, slightly rough against her bare arm. She loved him, loved him desperately. She couldn't begin to imagine life without him. She felt that she would die a little bit each day she was away from him. She loved him when he was happy, when he was excited, when he was somber, even when he was cold and stubborn—and angry. She loved him as a friend, as a lover, even as the stranger he could become when his mind was set, when he turned away from her, as he had now.

At eleven-thirty on the nose, their flight landed. Jeff led her off of the plane. Then, in the middle of the hallway, with people rushing all around them, he paused and stared at her.

"Well? Are we having lunch—or getting married?"

It was so different from the sweet proposal she longed for. His eyes were like ice chips, as uncompromising as his stance.

But, oh, she was so pathetically in love. She couldn't even think of letting him go. Suddenly she felt nothing but the thrill of excitement. Marriage...marriage...she'd be his wife. For a dizzying moment, she couldn't believe it. Couldn't believe that he loved her so very much, that she would really be able to touch him, sleep with him, love him...forever.

Jade lowered her eyes and hurried past him.

"We're getting married," she replied, her answer as curt as his question. She didn't have the nerve to look into his eyes again, so she kept walking in a tremendous hurry, totally unaware of where she was going.

He caught up with her, placing a hand on her back. He didn't speak, but she could have sworn his hand trembled.

They were out of the airport in seconds. Downtown in minutes. And before twelve noon, they were holding a legal license to be married.

They still hadn't spoken, not to each other. The only words they'd uttered had been their stiff answers to the clerk filling out the application.

When they left the courthouse, Jeff finally spoke to her. "This is it. Do we, or don't we? It's your very last out."

Jade couldn't breathe. It couldn't really be happening. She wasn't really about to marry him. What about Diana and Ryan?

She forced Diana and both children from her mind in a sudden spirit of recklessness. Today...these few hours...were hers.

She didn't know that she lifted her chin, that her eyes took on an emerald sparkle of challenge, or that the Atlanta wind gave her hair a wild and abandoned beauty all its own.

"Let's do it," she whispered.

Moments later, they were standing before the justice of the peace. She heard herself saying the words of the marriage ceremony, heard Jeffrey saying them beside her. He hadn't had a chance to buy a diamond or a wedding band; it was his college class ring that he slipped on her finger.

It was huge and threatened to fall off any second.

"With this ring..."

It didn't matter at all that the ring was too big, that their surroundings were less than romantic.

She was suddenly, legally, really and truly married to him.

Chapter 11

He felt like throwing his hat in the air, except that he didn't have a hat. It was done; they were married. Her fingers were shaking in his hand, and he felt just like primitive man, triumphant, and terribly possessive and territorial. She was his wife.

"Kiss the bride," the justice of the peace intoned. He did, with absolute pleasure, love and desire.

The Justice cleared his throat; Jeff ignored him.

Despite his joy, he was feeling a little guilty at the way he had threatened Jade. It had all been a bluff. No matter what she had said or done, he never would have let her out of his life. He'd been adamant because he was convinced that their being together was the very best way to handle the problems they faced. No matter how difficult their days, they would have the privacy of their bedroom at night, each other to cling to, touch and love.

Lord, he loved her so much. He loved the soft feel of her hair against his fingers, the color of her eyes, lush like a meadow, the sound of her voice. He loved her mind, loved watching her face as she thought things through. He loved her gentleness and her temper; her loved her honesty. He loved to kiss her, the way he was doing now. . . .

"Mr. Martin . . ."

The justice of the peace finally caught Jeff's attention. Laughing, Jeff released Jade, thanked the man, paid him and dragged Jade back out to the street.

She was flushing, a bright shade of red. Her lips were damp and swollen from his kiss, her eyes sparkling with outrage.

"How could you do that to me? Jeff, they were all staring at us! How—"

"Easy, Mrs. Martin, easy!" Mrs. Martin. His wife. He laughed out loud again and swept her back into his arms. Pedestrians walking by them stopped to stare and smile.

"Jeff!" she protested at last, breathless as she pulled herself away from him. "Jeff, we're on a public street—"

"Then let's get off it," he said huskily. "Unless you want lunch. No, we'd better not. I might wind up attacking you on a tablecloth . . ."

He was so glad to see her giggle. When she laughed the outrage disappeared from her eyes. She slipped her hands around his neck and leaned against him, still laughing. "We haven't any time; we've got a flight back to Miami in a matter of hours—"

"A matter of hours? Hell, woman, give me fifteen minutes and you'll remember it for a lifetime, I swear."

"Egotist," she accused him.

"With a one-track mind," he agreed."

"Jeff!"

"Let's go. I've got to make love to my wife. Now."

He already had a room reservation, she discovered, at a spectacular hotel in the Peachtree Center.

The door was barely closed behind them before his hands were on the zipper of her dress. "What time is it?" he asked.

She tried to glance at her watch, which was difficult, since her arms were caught in the dress he was slipping off her body.

"One forty-five."

"Umm. The champagne is due at two. We've got time."

"Time? You mean that someone is coming to this door in fifteen mintues? Jeffrey Martin, you leave my clothing alone—"

"Gladly. As soon as it's no longer on your body."

"Jeff—room service will be here—"

"In fifteen minutes. I told you, a lot can happen in fifteen minutes."

"Oh, you conceited—"

She tried to escape him and tripped over her dress. Jade winced, hoping that it wouldn't rip. She hadn't anything else to wear.

"Jeff—"

"Shh! You're wasting time!" Her shoes, panty hose, slip, bra and panties followed her dress to the floor, all despite her intent to stop him. She was laughing breathlessly when he lifted her to the bed and shed his own clothing in a flash, sending his jacket flying in one direction, his shirt in another, his pants in still another. For a moment he stood before her, regally, wonderfully male. Then he plunged down beside her, like a diver into the ocean, and her giggles were stilled by the damp heat of his mouth. Surrender came to her quickly as his closeness filled her with warmth and instant longing.

Fifteen minutes . . . fifteen minutes of hunger and awe. His body merged with hers, weaving a magical spell about the two of them. Their movements were like a dance, the cadence of their breathing and heartbeats like the music for that dance.

Fifteen minutes . . . and the cad was right. . . . The egotistical cad was right; she *would* remember them all her life. She would remember how she had gasped in exquisite pleasure just as there was a tap at the door. She would remember how smugly he smiled as he met her eyes, how he laughed when she desperately fought free of his weight and disappeared into the bathroom, slamming the door behind her.

Seconds later he joined her there. He was stark naked, carrying a silver tray of champagne and glasses in his hands, his dark hair tousled over his forehead, his crooked grin in place.

"You didn't—you didn't answer the door like that!" Jade asked, shocked.

"Well, of course." He set the tray on the tiled floor and started the water running in the huge tub.

"You didn't!"

"Well, all right, I didn't."

She was laughing again, giggling while he filled the tub, and still chortling when he deposited her in it and joined her. He told her to drink the champagne, and she tried to. But he was sudsing her body, causing her laughter to turn to gasps. Eventually, she put her glass down and clung to him while his fingers moved along her thighs and between them.

She couldn't smile or speak when he suddenly lifted her from the tub, water sluicing from them both. She could only hold onto him, staring into the intensity of his eyes as he carried her back to the bed. He didn't join her though. He disappeared and returned with the champagne.

"I've always wanted to do this," he said, pouring a tiny stream of champagne onto her belly. She gasped.

"Jeff—that's Dom Perignon!"

"I want to taste it . . . all over your body."

"Jeff . . ." She started to giggle again, but cried out instead. The tip of his tongue was moving where the champagne had been. He touched her, laved her breasts and her thighs, her toes, kneecaps, throat . . . the most intimate of places. All the while he whispered how much he loved her and reminded her that she was his wife. She couldn't remain still; she wanted to share the champagne with him . . . his way. Time stood still; it was measured by the beat of their pulses, the heavy rasp of their breathing, the incoherent things they murmured. At last they came together with tender ferocity. The explosion within her was so intense that Jade screamed. She felt as if she were surrounded first by soaring light, and then pitched into darkness. She trembled as the world at last ceased to spin, and she lay there, amazed that such ecstasy could really exist.

"My wife. Oh, God, Jade, I do love you so much."
His fingers moved in her hair, tenderly, gently.

"Oh, Jeff... I love you."

He kissed her, stroked her cheeks, stared into her
eyes. Then he sighed and rolled away, rising, stretching. She stared at the marvelous line of his shoulders,
back and buttocks.

"We've got a plane to catch," he said softly, and
disappeared into the bathroom.

They made the airport—and their plane—on time.

"When we land," Jeff told Jade, "I'll take you to
your car. You can get Sean from Toby's, run by your
house for a few things, then come back to the
Grange."

His fingers were curled easily around hers, but he
was smoking. That meant he was nervous. Jade's
stomach quivered uneasily.

She was his wife; there could be no going back. The
afternoon had shown her just how wonderful love
could be. But now, though she despised herself for it,
she was afraid again. Afraid of facing a nine-year-old
boy, and even more afraid of that child's mother.

"Maybe," Jade muttered softly, "it would be better if we kept our marriage a secret for a while. If I just
went home—"

"No deal! Absolutely no dice!" Jeff grated out
harshly, reminding her that the tender lover she had
married could also be a hard man, dangerous when
crossed. "If you aren't back at the house by nine
o'clock, I'll be out looking for you."

"But Ryan—"

"Ryan is my child. I am the parent. I can't let him
run my life."

"How will you feel," Jade asked, "if your child decides to go live with his mother? He's nine years old. Diana just might be able to walk into a courtroom and ask for custody if Ryan starts to say he wants to live with her."

"That's my problem," Jeff said curtly.

"Your problem? We're married now—"

"Don't worry about it!" he snapped. "Trust me— no court in the world would give her custody."

There was a sudden distance between them, and it hadn't disappeared by the time the plane landed. Jade ached, knowing that she loved him with her heart, but fearing that their hurried marriage had been a mistake.

A mistake? It was too late if it was. The deed was done; she was his wife. Wife. She mouthed the word. It was still a little unbelievable.

It was dark when he dropped her off at her car. "I mean it, Jade," he warned. "Nine o'clock. Talk to Sean and be there by then, or I'll come out and bring you home myself."

"Hey, you're my husband, not my keeper," she reminded him lightly. He didn't laugh, nor did he acknowledge the difference.

"Nine o'clock, Jade."

His Lincoln disappeared down the street. Jade sighed nervously and drove a little slowly to Toby's.

When she pulled into his driveway, both he and Lynn were waiting. They rushed out and kissed her. Sean followed more slowly, frowning, and Jade knew he hadn't been told anything, but that he was suspicious.

She thanked Toby and Lynn, smiled at Sean as he seated himself next to her and told him cheerfully that she'd have some news for him as soon as she reached the house.

"I know. You married him, didn't you?"

He was looking straight ahead, through the windshield and into the night. Jade couldn't tell what he was thinking or feeling.

"I—yes, Sean, I did. I meant to tell you before...before we actually did it. There were problems—"

"I know. Ryan. I hate that kid."

"Sean—"

Sean turned to her angrily. "Didn't you hear him! How can you defend him, Mom, after everything he said?"

They weren't anywhere near home, but Jade pulled off the road, anyway, and took him into her arms.

"Oh, Sean. Yes, I heard him. But don't you understand? That wasn't Ryan talking. He's hurt, and he's confused—"

"Because of his mother."

"Sean," she said, smoothing back his wonderful corn-colored hair and searching his eyes in the glow of the street lights. "You have to kind of look at it all from a distance, or go a little crazy," she admitted. "I don't think that Diana is really a bad person. She's just very beautiful and accustomed to getting what she wants. Jeff doesn't love her anymore; and she doesn't know how to deal with it, so she uses Ryan. Can you understand that?"

He had tears in his eyes; he lowered his head.

"My father wouldn't have been like that."

Jade hugged him closely, wondering just how much he had fathomed about her and Danny.

"No, he wouldn't have been," she said.

"You loved him, didn't you?"

"With all my heart."

That was true. She had loved Danny. Really loved him. And it was true, too, that Danny never would have used Sean to manipulate her the way Diana was using Ryan.

"What do you think?" she asked her son. "I mean—"

"I like Jeff. I like him a lot. It'll be kind of like having a real live hero for a stepfather. Like a dream."

"Oh, I'm so glad, Sean—"

"But I hate Ryan!"

"Sean! Please—" she began, but he interrupted her quickly.

"I'm not going to do anything. As long as he's okay to me, I'll be okay to him."

"Sean—"

"Are we moving in tonight?" he asked her, changing the subject. He wasn't about to promise her any more.

"Yes," she said, and put the Corvette into gear once more.

"I love the Grange," Sean remarked. "It's really neat." He was quiet for a minute. "And big. Ryan and I should be able to stay out of each other's way."

It took Jade longer than she'd expected to pick up the few things she needed for the night. Still it was only 9:05 when she pulled into the long driveway at the Grange

Apparently Jeff had meant his threat seriously. He was out in front, just about to slide into the driver's seat of the Lincoln.

He smiled when he saw her, though, and came around to help carry bags and parcels out of the car.

"Hi, Sean. I take it your mom talked to you. How do you feel about things?"

Sean grinned. "Fine, sir."

"Good, I'm glad," Jeff said, leading the way to the front door. He glanced at Jade. "Why don't you take your stuff on up to our bedroom. I'll show Sean his. Then he can have some hot chocolate and head for bed, since tomorrow's a school day."

"I—" Jade hesitated uneasily. She wasn't sure if she wanted Sean and Jeff alone together right now.

"Uh, where's Ryan?" she asked.

"In bed already," Jeff replied briefly. "Go on up, Jade. I'll take care of Sean. Mattie is in the kitchen if you need her for anything."

She smiled a little weakly, then started up the stairs, longing to be with the two of them, praying that things would go smoothly. She knew that Jeff and Sean would have to be alone together sometime. It was a beginning to making things work, to making the magic real.

In the bedroom, she stood before the tower window and felt the winter's breeze from the bay. She smiled slowly, thinking of the day when she'd stood here, and he had challenged her to make love to him.

Strange, that the house should feel so cold tonight, that after all the passion of the afternoon, there could be such tension between them.

The breeze touched her face again, seemed to caress her cheeks. It would be okay. It would be okay when they were together again. They would make it work.

Jeff didn't have any problems with Sean at all. Sean seemed quite impressed by the size of his room, and quite pleased by the view from his window, which looked out on the bay.

"I'll bet you can see boats out there a lot, huh?"

"Umm. Almost all the time," Jeff agreed. "We can get a boat if you want, but we'll have to be careful. I don't know much about sailing."

"Mom does," Sean assured him. "My dad loved boats. They used to sail a lot. You don't have to go far to go conching or fishing."

"Sounds nice," Jeff said.

"It is!" Sean said enthusiastically. "You mean, we can really get a boat?"

"Sure. We've got a dock out back."

"Wow," Sean said, sinking down on his bed.

Jeff smiled. "Why don't you go on down and ask Mattie for hot chocolate now. It's getting later and later."

Sean nodded and then looked at him a little defiantly. "I don't have to change my name, do I? There's nothing wrong with yours, it's just that—well, you're not my father. And I ... he ..."

"You don't have to change your name. I know that you loved your father very much. His name is yours. No one can take that away from you. You'll always have him—you just have me, too, now."

Jeff grinned, then started to leave the bedroom. Sean called him back. "Hey, Jeff?"

"Hmm?"

"That's it?"

"What's it?"

Sean squirmed a little. "Aren't you going to give me a . . . a lecture, or something? Like how I have to listen to you, toe the line and all that stuff."

Jeff hesitated a second. He lowered his eyes, smiled again, then forced himself to put on a serious expression.

"No, Sean, I'm not going to give you any lectures. You've always listened to me before. And you're old enough to use common sense. We'll just see how things go, huh?"

"Yeah. Yeah, I guess."

Jeff started to leave again; Sean called him back again. "Jeff?"

"Yeah?"

"Ryan and me . . . we don't get along very well, you know."

"Ryan will learn to shape up" was all that Jeff said. He left, and Sean didn't call him back again.

"I'm glad I'm not in your shoes, Ryan Martin," Sean mumbled aloud to himself.

At ten o'clock, Jeff, Jade and Sean were sitting out by the pool drinking hot chocolate. Jeff decided he was hungry; Jade said that she wasn't. But as soon as Mattie brought Jeff a thinly sliced steak sandwich, Jade found it smelled delicious, and ate half of it. Sean laughed as the two of them argued playfully over the sandwich. Mattie sighed maternally and came back shortly with another plate of sandwiches. Finally, even Sean, who'd had pork roast already at Toby's, found that he was starving.

It was eleven when they went up to bed. Sean walked past Ryan's door and wondered unhappily if his new stepbrother had been watching them or if he had cried himself to sleep. Sean wanted to feel triumphant; he didn't. He just felt sorry for Ryan.

Jade felt even worse. When they were behind the closed door of their tower room, she turned quickly to Jeff.

"Jeff, what happened with Ryan?"

He shrugged out of his shirt, grimacing as he went to toss it in the hamper in the bathroom.

"Nothing," he said at last.

"What do you mean, nothing?" Jade persisted.

"Just what I said. Nothing."

"Damn you, Jeff, don't shut me out of this."

He sighed, continuing to strip. "I'm not shutting you out, Jade. It's just that nothing happened. I told him that you and I had gotten married, and that if he didn't like it, I was sorry. He didn't say anything at all. He asked if he could go to bed, and I said fine."

His clothing was all off. He looked fantastic nude, Jade decided a little resentfully. He seemed so comfortable and natural, smiling as he paused in front of her and started removing her clothing.

"Jeff—" She tried to turn to face him, but his grip on her zipper prevented it. Its rasp interrupted the flow of her words. "Jeff...Jeff, I feel so awful. Maybe one of us should have gone to his room. We need to tread gently with him." She stepped out of her dress, able to face him at last.

He shook his head. "I think it's better to let him come to us. If we beg him to join us, he'll feel that he's winning. Then he'll just turn away more. If we ignore him, he'll come out of his shell eventually."

Was Jeff right? She didn't know.

"I feel so guilty..." she muttered.

His hands were on her again, stripping away the last of her clothing. With long strides he carried her to the bed that was now—miraculously—half hers. Married. They'd gotten married today. She was his wife.

"The thing that I feel guilty about is gypping you out of a honeymoon," he said, kissing her deeply, then spreading her hair out on the pillow.

She felt happy again. Secure... and excited. "We didn't really need a honeymoon," she replied. "This is surely the most beautiful place on earth," she said huskily. "I have you, the sea breeze, this lovely room..."

"My feelings exactly," he told her. "Eden, my love, exists wherever you walk. Or lie, actually."

"Ouch! That sounds decadent."

"I love being decadent."

"Well, this is certainly decadent. I can't imagine making love so many times in one day. It seems... illicit. Immoral. Definitely decadent."

"It seems like a hell of a lot of fun to me," Jeff said, correcting her with a husky chuckle. The things he said next were far more than decadent. They were hoarse and guttural, and they elicited a passion that did indeed make an Eden of their tower room.

She rested later, happy in his arms. She moaned slightly when he moved against her again, and accused him once more of decadence. He reminded her that it was their wedding night and said they were supposed to be decadent. Again she laughed, and before long her laughter became gasps, then whimpers and moans.

She knew it was about four o'clock when she finally dozed off. She remembered seeing the time on her luminous wristwatch as she fell asleep, contented in his arms.

When the phone started ringing, she happened to catch sight of the time again. It was 5:00.

Jeff swore slightly and told her to go back to sleep. He would take the call in the den.

"Who would call at this time of night?" she asked him with a yawn? He didn't answer her, and she was so exhausted that she fell back to sleep without pressing the point.

The next thing she knew, there was an obnoxious buzzing sound in her ear; as she came slowly awake, she realized that it was the alarm sounding.

Maybe it was a good thing she couldn't find the off switch right away, because she would have gone back to sleep. By the time she found the right button, she was wide awake. Wide awake, frowning with a headache, and wondering where on earth Jeff had gone. He was nowhere to be found in the bedroom, bathroom or den.

Muttering beneath her breath, she quickly showered, dressed, and raced down the stairs. She found Mattie in the kitchen. Mattie, bless her capable heart, instantly handed Jade a cup of tea. Not coffee—tea. Jeff had apparently advised Mattie about Jade's habits.

"Where's Jeff?" she asked the housekeeper.

"I really don't know," Mattie replied cheerfully, turning back to her frying pan of fluffy scrambled eggs. "He must have gone out quite early. Breakfast is just about ready. Where are those boys?"

"I'll call them," Jade said. She went back to the foot of the stairs, annoyed at the nervousness she felt at the prospect of seeing Ryan, and furious with Jeff for leaving her to do it alone.

"Ryan! Sean! Come on down for breakfast. And hurry—you'll be late for school!"

"Coming!" Sean called down to her.

Ryan gave no answer.

Jade wandered back into the kitchen. "What will you have, dear?" Mattie asked her.

"Just the tea right now, thanks."

Ryan appeared in the doorway, his eyes downcast. Silently, he took a seat at the counter.

"Morning, young man," Mattie said cheerfully.

"Morning," Ryan mumbled.

Sean appeared next. He kissed his mother, gazed at the place setting arranged for him next to Ryan, hesitated, stiffened, but then got onto his stool. "Hi, Ryan."

"Hi," Ryan returned.

"I think I'll find the newspaper," Jade said. She went outside, annoyed to find it on the lawn, which probably meant that Jeff had left really early since he hadn't brought it in.

She went back to the kitchen. Mattie was chatting about the nice weather. "What an improvement," she told Jade with a wink. "When I left Chicago there was a wind chill factor of thirty below. I'm going to like this place."

Jade smiled. Sean told Mattie that he wished he could see snow. Just once, he'd like to be able to build a snowman.

"I've never made a snowman in my whole life."

"It's not all that it's cracked up to be," Ryan answered.

Well, at least he's talking to Sean, if not to me, Jade thought. She glanced at her watch. It was getting late. She hesitated. Ryan was in a private school; Sean was in public classes. She wondered whether they should go to the same school from now on; maybe it was a good thing that they didn't.

"Sean, come on. We have to go. Ryan, do you want me to take you in?"

He didn't look at her, but he answered her civilly. "No, thank you. The bus will come."

"Okay," Jade said. "Sean, let's go."

She dropped him off at school, then decided to stop by her own house for a few more things. It was about ten when she came back to the Grange; she noted that the Lincoln was back in front of the house, and her temper quickened. She wanted to rip out a handful of Jeff's hair for leaving her alone that morning.

The door slammed behind her as she entered the house. Mattie came running out to the foyer.

"Oh, there you are; Jeff was just asking for you."

"Where is he?" Jade asked tensely.

"Up in the den."

"Thanks."

Jade stomped up the steps and into the den. Jeff was behind his desk. He was in a suit, and he looked tired and strained as he leaned back in the chair. He wasn't doing anything but rubbing his temples with his thumb and forefinger. He winced and opened his eyes as Jade appeared before him.

"Where the hell did you go?" she demanded. He looked at her, but didn't answer, and she couldn't begin to interpret the dark emotion in his eyes. "Jeff, where did you go? You had no right to leave me here alone this morning. Especially this morning."

Still he hesitated.

"Jeff?"

"Out," he said harshly, closing his eyes again and pressing his temples.

She felt a tingling sensation, a warning of some fear she hadn't acknowledged as yet.

"Out where?"

He sighed.

I should lie, he warned himself. I should lie like hell. But he didn't want to lie. He loved the honesty between them too much.

"Sit down, Jade," he suggested.

"I don't think I want to sit down," she said warily. "Jeff, where were you?"

He stood and walked over to the mullioned window.

"That phone call this morning was from an old friend of mine. A guy named Darby Moran. Ever heard of him?"

"No," Jade said flatly.

Jeff shrugged with a vague motion. "He used to play for the Bruins. He retired a few years ago, and does commercials for motor oil down here now."

"What," Jade asked stiffly, "does Darby Moran, the motor oil salesman, have to do with you walking out in the middle of our wedding night?"

Jeff winced. "He was, ah, at a party."

"At 5:00 a.m.?"

"Yeah. A lot of sports types were there. You know, they play hard on the field, and then they play hard off it."

"No, I don't know. But go on."

He hesitated, staring straight out the window.

"Diana was there, too."

Jade inhaled sharply.

"You coerced me into marrying you at the drop of a hat, then on the very night that we were married, you ran out to be with your ex-wife?"

"No!" He replied sharply, spinning around. Her face was deathly pale; her eyes were sparkling like emeralds. He started walking toward her, but she put a hand in the air and backed away.

He stopped, praying he could make her understand.

"Jade, it wasn't like that at all. I still don't know who she went to this party with. But she was a mess. Darby called to warn me that she might very well kill herself and a number of other people if she drove in her condition. He would have taken her home himself except that his wife threatened him with a divorce if he did. Diana can be threatening to other women."

"Yes, she can, can't she?" Jade said sweetly. Then she spun around and walked out of the room, on fire with pain and anger. She was barely aware of what she was doing.

"Jade!" he thundered.

She was halfway down the stairs when he started after her. She was moving quickly. By the time he got outside, she was in the Corvette.

"Where are you going?"

"Home," she answered vaguely.

"This is your home."

"No. It isn't." She turned the key in the ignition. Jeff swore furiously and reached in, grabbing the keys from her fingers.

She bolted out of the car and started down the walk. He ran after her.

"Jade listen to me—" he began, clutching her arm.

"No!" She wrenched her arm from his grasp and kept going.

"Jade!"

His voice bellowed after her, but she just kept going.

This time when he caught her, she couldn't escape him. He swung her into his arms, and ignored her flailing fists as he stalked back toward the house.

"Damn you, Jeffrey Martin, you have not become my master! You can't make things a certain way by strength alone! I will not live here with you when you keep going back to her! I won't do it, I won't do it, I won't do it!"

He kept walking.

"Let me down! Where are you taking me?"

"Back to our bedroom."

"You son of a—"

"You married me, Jade. For better or worse."

"Jeff—"

"You can listen to me, and then we can make love. Or we can make love, and then you can listen to me. But you married me, and damn you, I will *not* let you run away from it."

Chapter 12

They made love first.

Ridiculously, against all logic, they made love. Thirty minutes later, staring blankly at the ceiling above her, hugging her pillow close, Jade morosely wondered why it had been so easy. Was there such a fine line between anger and desire? Or was it that just that they were newlyweds, new lovers?

It was frightening to her. Very frightening. Because if she found herself in his arms so easily, wouldn't it be possible for him to find himself, held just so, by Diana? Hating her, yet wanting her?

"Jade, don't you see?"

He had been talking to her for the past five minutes, explaining. She'd barely heard his voice. But now, something of the desperation in it touched her, drew her attention.

"I had to go this time. It might very well have been a ploy to get my attention, but I had to go, anyway. It's an old trick of hers. She's always known that I'd come because of Ryan. That was part of the reason I left Chicago—I didn't think she'd call for help if I was far away. I never thought that she might come down here."

Jade swallowed painfully, determined not to look at him, determined to keep her voice cold. "So every time she gets a little too loaded to drive, you're going to go and get her. For Ryan's sake, of course. And I'm supposed to understand."

He ran his fingers through his hair impatiently. "No. I said that I had to go—this time. I picked her up, got her into my car and drove her back to her hotel. Then I poured coffee into her and told her that I didn't understand why I had suddenly become the passion of her life again, but that it didn't matter. I told her I was in love with you and that we were married. I also told her that nothing she could say or do would change that."

She rolled to her side, fighting tears.

"Jade."

"What?"

"Talk to me, answer me."

"I don't know what to say."

"Can you understand?"

"No! No!" she cried vehemently, rolling back over and facing him. "I can't! I'm not Pollyanna! I don't want her to have this hold on you!"

"She has no hold on me! If you trusted me—"

"I trust you! I just don't want you alone with her."

He swore and stalked over to the window. The sunlight spilled gold over his hard, muscled body. Jade hopped out of the bed and hurried toward the bathroom. Jeffrey swung around abruptly, catching her arm.

"Where are you going?"

"To take a shower."

"And then?"

"I'm going in to work."

"You don't have to go to work. Sandy isn't expecting you."

"I've decided that I definitely want to keep my job."

He paused for a second, watching her. "That's good. Maybe you can start by putting your house on the market."

"My house? I don't want to sell it!"

"You don't need it."

"I bought it as an investment. It's Sean's, if he ever wants or needs it."

"Or yours—anytime you want to run away."

"I *don't* want to run away. I just don't want to share my husband with his ex-wife!"

"You're not leaving!"

She closed her eyes, unconsciously twisting her wrist in his grasp.

"Jade! I mean it."

"Jeff, let go—"

He pulled her closer to him, then the anger was gone, and he smoothed the hair at her nape. "By God, I swear it, Jade, I love you. Promise me that you won't run out."

She stiffened for a moment, fighting the persuasion of his voice, the power of his hold. Then she gave up, leaning against him weakly.

"I'm not running out on you," she said.

"Jade . . ." He kissed the top of her head.

"Not . . . not now. But I can't handle this situation, Jeff. I may be insecure, I don't know. But if you ever leave me for her again, I will be gone. Do you understand?"

"I understand just one thing," he told her fiercely. "That I will never, never let you go. Any time you try to leave me, I will bring you back."

"Jeff—"

"Jade! I told you why I went this one time. It isn't going to happen again." He kissed the top of her head. "Go on, take your shower. Go to work. Maybe I should have drawn up a prenuptial agreement before we married. I never thought of it because I didn't want any outs. I didn't need any insurance policies, but it seems that you do."

"Jeff—"

"Never mind. If you don't want the first shower, I do."

He walked into the bathroom and slammed the door. Jade wanted to cry. She wanted to storm into the bathroom and tell him that she'd happily quit her job and sell her house, anything to make them happy, anything to close the distance between them.

But she didn't. She waited, and when he came out, she showered and dressed and went to work.

For a day that had begun so horribly, the evening was surprisingly pleasant. She'd forgotten about Little League, but Sean reminded her when she picked him up at school.

And when they arrived at practice, she discovered that Toby had a surprise for them. Alcoholic beverages were strictly forbidden on the field, but Toby and Lynn had arranged for a surprise party at their house to celebrate Jade and Jeff's marriage. Everyone came—all the parents and all the kids—and it was wonderful. Everyone wished Jeff and Jade all the happiness in the world. Even the kids thought it was romantic.

Jade couldn't help being touched by the warmth around her. Nor could Jeff. When their eyes met across Toby's living room, they both smiled, and peace was instantly declared between them.

Sean walked around looking very proud. And though Ryan had nothing good to say, he refrained from stating his true opinion of the situation.

When they all returned home, Ryan started straight up the stairs.

"Ryan!" Jeff called sharply.

Ryan paused, turning back warily.

"Aren't you going to say good-night?" Jeff demanded.

"Good night," Ryan said, after a brief pause. Then he continued up the stairs.

Jade went to kiss Sean good-night after he had taken his shower, done his homework and crawled into bed. As she passed by Ryan's door, she heard him sobbing softly. She placed her hand on his doorknob, but then hesitated and continued down the hall. In her own bedroom, she asked Jeff to go in and say good-night to him.

"If he wants to be a brat," Jeff said stubbornly, "let him be a brat."

"Jeff, that's not fair. He's a nine-year-old boy. He loves both his parents, and he's hurt."

Jeff threw a shoe into the corner of the room. "He loves both his parents," he spat out bitterly. "He'd have been left in a gutter if it was up to his mother. She used to leave him with anyone at any time to go out and party. I'm the only one who's ever cared for that kid. When he was a baby, I was the one up at two in the morning. *I* changed his diapers; *I* sat with him through his fevers and colds; *I* was there. And now he hates *me* and turns to *her*!"

"Jeff, Jeff...listen to yourself!" Jade pleaded, kneeling beside him. "Jeff, he's too young to understand all that. All he knows is that you are both his parents. My God, yes, you sacrificed for him. But you did that because you loved him, not because you expected the reward of his love. Jeff, please, think about what you just said."

He stared at her. His eyes widened slowly. He touched her hair, smoothing it against her cheek. "Now I know why I love you so much," he murmured softly.

He stood then and left the room. An hour later, when he still wasn't back, Jade tiptoed down the hall. Ryan's door was open, and Jade went in.

Jeff was sound asleep beside Ryan. Tears were still drying upon Ryan's cheeks, but his arms were wound tightly around his father.

Jade pulled a light blanket over the two of them, and tiptoed out of the room smiling. Jeff had left her on the second night of their marriage, too, but she didn't mind at all. Not when he had left her for his son.

Three weeks followed, three weeks of such searing happiness that Jade couldn't believe her good fortune. Ryan still didn't speak to her much, but he and Sean were getting on well enough, and his relationship with his father was almost back to normal. Jade was starting to hope that the four of them might make it together as a family, after all.

That hope died exactly twenty-one days after her marriage to Jeff.

It was night, a cold night. Though it was almost March a freak cold spell had come in, threatening frost. They'd had a fire burning downstairs and they'd toasted marshmallows and prepared hot chocolate. Then, sitting in front of the blaze, everyone had told ghost stories.

The boys had gone to bed, and Mattie had retired for the night. Jeff was just going to lockup the house, and then they'd be alone together in their bedroom.

Filled with the wonderful excitement of being in love, Jade rushed into the shower, and bathed herself with scented soap. Then she put on a silky nightgown and dived between the sheets to await her husband.

When the phone started ringing, it didn't bother her; it didn't occur to her that anything could disturb her happiness. But when half an hour had gone by, and Jeff still hadn't come up, she began to worry.

A shivering started inside her. She got up and slipped into a robe, then started down the spiral stairway.

He was just getting into a jacket, ready to leave.

"Jeff!" she rasped. He stared at her. He looked pale and haggard, and very weary.

"It was Diana!" she cried. "And you're going!" she screamed a little hysterically. "You're going!"

"Jade!" he said sharply.

But she wouldn't listen. "Go! Go! But dammit, I won't be here waiting this time!"

"Jade!" he called again, but she didn't wait. She sped back up the stairs and locked herself into their room, then pitched herself on the bed and gave in to a fit of wild and desperate tears. Surely he would come to her. He would try the doorknob. He wouldn't leave...

He didn't leave. The bedroom door slammed inward with terrible force, and he appeared in the doorway. She felt as if her heart had stopped.

She had never seen him look so forbidding, so haggard and remote. She could have sworn that he hated her as he stood there, staring at her.

There was something very wrong. She had been fighting for herself, for their love, for the future of their marriage. At that awful shattering sound of the door, she had, for one brief second, thought that she might have gotten through to him. She had thought that he understood why she couldn't keep trusting him when he continued to leave her.

But she knew before he spoke that he had not come to apologize, to promise that he would stand at her side.

"I have to go—"

"So go!" she whispered furiously.

"Diana is dead," he said flatly.

Jade couldn't speak. She stared at him with slowly dawning comprehension and horror.

"No...."

He turned then and left her. A moment later, she heard his steps on the stairway. She sprang from the bed and raced after him in the worst agony of remorse and sorrow she had ever known.

"Jeff!"

He didn't stop when she called his name. With tears stinging her eyes once more, she fled down the stairs, catching his arm at the landing. He stopped and stared down at her, but there was no sign of emotion whatsoever in his eyes or rigid features.

"Jeff...Jeffrey, I'm so sorry! Oh, my God, I'm sorry. I didn't know, I didn't understand—"

He shook his arm free of her hold. "No, and you still don't understand, do you? You never have. You've never trusted me, and you've never believed in me. I was the fool to ever hope that you could. It doesn't matter."

"Jeff—" Desperately, she reached out to him again.

"Jade, I have to go identify the body. She wrapped herself around a tree in that car of hers. Then I'm going to have to break it to Ryan."

"I'll go with you—"

"No, you won't."

"Jeff, let me go with you. Don't go alone. I'm so sorry—"

"And I'm sorry, too, Jade, because your apology doesn't mean anything at all to me right now. I just want to be left alone."

He walked out the front door. It closed softly behind him, and that quiet sound was far worse than any thunder she'd ever heard.

"Oh, God, no," Jade whispered. Shaking, she stumbled into the kitchen and poured herself a brandy. Diana was dead. She couldn't be . . . but she was.

Ryan! Ryan would be so hurt. He was so young, and he had adored his mother.

Jade sank to the ground. If only there were something she could do. Oh, please, Lord, she thought. I know what this feels like. I would do anything to make it easier for them.

But Ryan despised her; he would never let her help. And Jeff . . . he hated her now.

She must have been on the floor a long time, longer than she had thought. The front door opened again and then closed. Jeff came into the kitchen, his jacket tossed over his shoulder. He saw her on the floor, but said nothing. He dropped his jacket over the counter, reached for a glass and poured himself a brandy. When he sat at the counter, she saw that his hands were shaking.

"Jeff—"

"Go to bed, Jade."

"I want to—"

"Go to bed. In the morning, I'll have to wake Ryan early. I'm taking Diana's body back to Chicago for interment in her family's plot. Ryan will come with me."

"Jeff, please, let me come—"

He shook his head. "Jade, I don't want you with me. Isn't that plain enough?"

She stood then and left the kitchen. She didn't go into their room, but went to Sean's, where she lay down beside her son. She needed his warmth and love. She thought that she would never sleep, so sorry was she for Diana, Ryan, Jeff and herself. Maybe she never had understood him. And now, it seemed that there was no future for the two of them.

She did sleep. When she awoke, she learned from a distraught Mattie that Jeff and Ryan had already left; Ryan had been sobbing so hard that Jeff had carried him out.

Jeff had left no message for her.

Jade decided not to send Sean to school that day. When she told him what had happened, he fell silent. Jade held him for a while, but then left him alone. His father's death was not a distant enough memory for Sean to have forgotten any of the pain.

Jade wandered around the house like a zombie. Eventually, Sean came down to talk to her.

"Mom—" he took her hands in his "—Mom, we should be there."

Tears that she couldn't control came to her eyes. "Sean, he ... Jeff ... doesn't want us there."

Sean sat with her a long, long time.

The weekend came and passed, and the two of them wandered around miserably, getting under Mattie's feet. Mattie urged them to go out and do something, but neither of them had the heart for it.

It wasn't until Tuesday afternoon that Jade went out—Sean decided that he wanted to go to baseball practice. It was there that Jade told Toby and Lynn the story of the night that Diana had died.

"You need to go to Chicago—now," Toby told her firmly when she had finished.

"Toby! He told me point-blank that he didn't want me!"

"After he had just identified the body of his son's mother. Maybe he did need a little time alone. But it's unhealthy for this to continue now, Jade. I know that he loves you. And if you love him and that little boy of his, you'll go up there. You'll just be there for him, waiting. Do it, Jade."

She listened to Toby, and she listened to her own heart.

Then she decided that she must go to Chicago. For Jeff, for Ryan, for herself and Sean, she had to go.

She didn't intend to take Sean—he'd seen enough of death for a child his age—but when they reached home and she explained that she was going to Chicago and that he would be staying with Toby for a few days, he vehemently opposed her.

"I'm going, too. I lost my father; I can help Ryan learn to live with the fact that he's lost his mother."

He looked so mature and wise as he stood there that Jade couldn't do anything but nod.

The following afternoon Sean still looked wise beyond his years as they stood before the door of Jeff's elegant Chicago town house. Jade stared at the door a long time. It was Sean who finally rang the bell.

It was answered by a tall woman, as stately and elegant as the house. She had silver hair and pleasant features that proudly displayed the creases of time.

"Yes?" she said, but before Jade could speak, she gasped slightly and pulled them in out of the snow.

"You're Jade! And you, young man, must be Sean."

"Uh, yes—"

The woman smiled a little sadly. "I'm your mother-in-law. My son was rude enough to remarry without informing me or his father, but he did at least tell us about you after the fact. Apparently he neglected to mention us."

Jade smiled uneasily, but the older woman seemed to have things in control.

"Get your coats off, both of you. Floridians." She sniffed. "Haven't the sense to get out of wet coats. My name is Frieda, by the way. Freddy, I'm afraid, to most people. I can't seem to shake that nickname, no matter how old I get."

"You're not old," Sean said with a bit of awe.

"Bless you, child," Frieda said, taking their coats, shaking them, and hanging them on hooks by the door. "Sean, you might benefit from a warm bath. Take your bag and go right up those stairs. Jade, you come with me, and we'll put some tea on."

Sean glanced at his mother, then obeyed Frieda. Jade followed the older woman as she led the way into a warm, comfortable kitchen.

"Jeffrey went out," she told Jade over her shoulder. She hesitated and then said, "He's at the cemetery. Diana was buried Monday. Ryan is in his room. Still crying his poor little eyes out, I'm afraid." Unhappily, she shook her head. "Jeff asked me to stay here for Ryan's sake, but I can't reach him right now— none of us can. I'm so glad you're here." She put a kettle on the stove and turned around to stare at Jade.

With her son's blunt candor, she asked, "What took you so long?"

Jade, unable to control herself any longer, burst into tears.

In the half hour that followed, Jade came to know and love her mother-in-law very well. She found herself telling Frieda the whole story and admitting that she was afraid Jeff would never forgive her for being jealous at such a time.

Frieda, with her arm around Jade, paused a minute, then sighed. "Nonsense, dear. I'm sure that Jeff came alone because...because he might have thought that this was something he had to do by himself. He's feeling guilty, of course. But that will pass. No one could have changed Diana. She liked life in the fast lane. Jeff will realize that, if he hasn't already."

"Ryan—" Jade gulped.

Frieda folded her hands in her lap. "Go talk to him."

"Me? You don't understand! He resents me—"

"You're exactly what he needs. Jade Martin, you're a big girl. You go up there and try. My grandson needs you."

She couldn't do it...she just couldn't do it. But with Frieda's prodding, she was on her feet and moving up the carpeted stairs.

And then, with a nod from Frieda, she was knocking on Ryan's door. No one answered. Frieda came to her, pushed the door open and then disappeared.

Jade swallowed back her own tears and moved into the room. It was dark; Ryan was sitting on his bed, staring out at the snow.

"I don't want anything to eat, Gram," he said dully.

"Ryan." Jade swallowed once again after she said his name. "It's me, Jade."

He swung around and stared at her, his huge blue eyes red and swollen from crying. His shoulders shook. He jumped to his feet, new tears streaming down his cheeks.

"You? I hate you, I hate you!" he cried. Then he ran at her, striking out wildly. "Go away, I hate you, I hate you..."

She caught his flailing arms; he had cried out all his strength. For a moment she wanted to flee, to do just as he told her.

She didn't. She closed her arms tightly around him, holding him to her. "I'm sorry, Ryan. I'm so very, very sorry."

He fell against her, no longer fighting her. She lifted him and carried him back to his bed, holding him as he continued to cry.

"You hated her; you wanted her to die!" he accused.

"No, Ryan, I didn't hate her. I'd never want anyone to die."

"But she's dead! Dead! Gone..."

"Shh, shh, shh." Jade started to mumble things, soothing things, anything she could think of.

"She wasn't bad! She wasn't bad!" Ryan moaned.

"Oh, no! She wasn't bad!" Jade told him, holding herself away from him so she could search his eyes. "Oh, honey, she wasn't bad at all. She was very beautiful, so beautiful. She had energy and vitality—"

"And she's in heaven, isn't she? Jade, isn't she?"

Jade was thoroughly convinced that if there was a God, He was truly all-seeing, and all-forgiving.

"Yes, Ryan. She's in heaven. She was beautiful and free, maybe too beautiful for this earth. She is in heaven now."

She stayed there for a long time rocking him. Once he pulled away from her.

"You're not her," he told her vehemently. "You're not my mother, and you never will be!"

"No, Ryan, I'm not. And I'll never try to be. But I am here, if you ever need me. If I can do anything."

He didn't answer her. Sometime later she realized that he had gotten very heavy. He had fallen asleep.

She laid him down gently and went downstairs.

She didn't have to say anything to Frieda. The older woman seemed to understand with a glance. She was busy at the moment with the little details of life, fixing Sean cocoa and a sandwich.

"I'll call you a taxi," Frieda said. "You can go and find Jeff."

"I . . . I won't know where I'm going," Jade said.

"I've got directions all written down for the cab driver," Frieda said, and then she was speaking into the phone, asking for a cab to come.

"Mom," Sean spoke up, "I'll go with you."

"No, you won't, young man," Frieda said cheerfully. "You'll stay right here. Ryan might come down, and I might need you."

It was just the right thing to say. He nodded. Jade still felt heartsick and numb. But under Frieda's competent direction, she found herself back in her coat, then sliding into the back seat of a taxi, handing directions to the taxi driver.

The cemetery seemed all too short a distance away. Before she knew it, before she was ready for it, she was there.

There was snow on the ground and on the gravestones. It seemed a truly bleak and lonely place.

"This is it, lady," the cabbie said.

She knew it was. She could see Jeff, a lone figure in a sheepskin coat, standing in the snow, staring downward. The white flakes fell against his dark hair; he held his hat in his fingers.

Jade got out of the cab. She heard it drive away. The snow was cold against her cheeks; she felt frozen, unable to move.

But at last she forced herself to do so. Plodding through the snow, she approached the man she loved.

Chapter 13

Jade walked slowly toward him, then paused, just steps away. It seemed so forlorn there. It was too soon for the tombstone to have been put in, and the soft flakes of snow had covered the ground, making the gravesite barely discernible. Jeff was so still, so very still. She was suddenly afraid to touch him, so she cleared her throat as she closed the distance between them.

He glanced up, as if from a deep reverie. Surprise flickered in his eyes as he saw her, but then it was gone, and he was just staring at her while the snow swirled between them. Jade felt as if her heart had ceased to beat, as if she had ceased to breathe.

And then he reached out a hand to her. He didn't speak, but a smile touched his lips. She accepted his hand gladly. He pulled her to him, and she rested her head against his coat, so very grateful for the warmth she found there.

"Jeff—" she tried to begin, but her voice was a rasp, like the winter's wind. "Jeff, I'm sorry. I had to come. I..."

He nodded, squeezing her hand. There was a bench not far behind them, a stone bench, as cold as the marble angels and trumpeters and tombs that filled the old cemetery. He led her there, and they sat.

"Oh, Jeff—" she began again miserably, but he interrupted her.

"I still can't believe it, you know. Diana was always so vital. But so damned wild. I suppose this was always coming. Still, I was just so shocked."

He was staring out at the white drifts of snow. Jade wasn't sure that he remembered she was there. She didn't know if he was talking to her, or just musing out loud.

"It's the strangest thing when something like this happens. We certainly weren't friends anymore. But there were so many years. I don't suppose that you can live with someone for that long and not feel the loss." He paused. "And then, of course, there's Ryan."

"Jeff—"

"I don't really understand it. I feel as though I've buried a part of my life, my youth perhaps."

Jade gripped his hands to draw his attention to her. "Jeff, I love you. I want to be with you. I want to help. I know that you didn't want me here, but please—"

He blinked, as if confused. "Jade, my love, I do want you here." He stroked her cheek with his gloved hand, as if really seeing her for the first time. "I'm sorry for the things I said the night Diana died. I felt so cold there for a while . . . doubly hurt, shocked—I don't really know what came over me. But I love you. I wouldn't have wished this upon you, but I'm glad you're here now. Very glad."

She was so relieved at his words that she started crying, and her words tumbled out. "Oh, God, Jeff . . . I was so frightened, so afraid that you wouldn't want me again . . . ever. You didn't call, you didn't—"

A slow smile curved his lips. "Jade." He said her name very softly, then reached out for her, drawing her into his arms.

"I swear you Southerners are all alike. You don't have enough sense to stay out of the snow," he said softly, his face pressed tenderly to her forehead. "Jade, I didn't call because you've already gone through something like this." He shrugged. "Maybe I was afraid, too. After the way I behaved toward you, I was afraid that you might not want to speak to me. I thought that I might be best to wait until I got home before I tried to explain."

"Oh, Jeff! Then you would have come back to me."

"Jade! Of course I would have come back. Did you think that I wouldn't? I only went because had to. I had to bury her. I owed her that much."

Jade sagged against him. "I was just so afraid," she said huskily. "I've always been afraid that you loved her. Really loved her beneath all the pain and anger."

He frowned. "How could you believe that?"

"She was so beautiful."

"Yes, she was beautiful, and maybe that's part of why this hurts so much. I didn't love her, Jade. That died long ago. But I was always a little sorry for her. She had so much to give; it seems a tragedy that she couldn't straighten out her life. There was good in Diana—there is in all people, I believe. She loved Ryan, even though she wasn't averse to hurting him to get her way. I don't know." He shuddered. "They told me that she died instantly, that she didn't feel a thing."

"Oh, Jeff. Can you believe me? I'm so very sorry. For everything."

"There's nothing for you to be sorry for."

"But—"

"You're shivering. Thin blood," he teased lightly. Then he was on his feet. "Come on. Let's get out of here."

He helped her stand.

"How did you get here?" he asked. "How did you find me?"

"I went to the house. Your mother gave me directions." Jade hesitated. "She's lovely, Jeff. You never told me anything about her."

He smiled, pausing in the snow to stare down at her and stroke her cheek again. "There's a lot we haven't had time to discover about each other yet."

He started walking again. "Is Sean here?"

"Yes, he's at the house."

"Have you seen Ryan?"

"Yes." She gazed up at his handsome profile, dark against the whiteness of the snow all around them.

"I think," she said slowly, "I think that Ryan and I will be all right together. With a little time. Healing . . . healing takes time."

"Yes, it does." He pointed ahead. "That's my car."

"The Jeep?"

"Yes."

"It would be. You like big cars."

She felt him shiver and knew it wasn't from the cold.

"We're getting rid of that Corvette of yours. It's a Fiberglas menace."

She didn't dispute with him. His words meant that they had a life together, a future.

They reached the Jeep and there he paused, pulling her tightly against him.

"You know," he said, "the terrible part of it all is that so much of what I feel is gratitude. I'm so very grateful to be alive. She is gone...her life snuffed out so easily. And it makes me feel that so many things are special: watching the sky, the sun, the snow, just seeing a snowflake. I have so much to be grateful for. I have you. We have our life together. Jade, I love you. I love you so much that it hurts at times. The important thing is that we have years and years together ahead of us. No matter what, through anger, laughter and even tears, we'll have each other."

She slipped her arms around his neck. She felt his breath, warm against her cold cheek. She felt the thunder of his heart against her chest, and here, in this place of frigid death, she felt joy as well as sorrow. He did love her as deeply as she loved him. There would have to be a time to mourn; that was a part of life.

But somewhere, there was sunshine, too. And they would find it together.

"Get in," he said huskily. "You're not used to this cold."

They drove back to his town house. Frieda was at the door, looking a little anxious.

"Where are the boys?" Jeff asked his mother.

She smiled, giving them a little sigh of relief.

"Out back, together."

Jeff raised his brows, pulled off his gloves and took Jade's hand. They walked to the kitchen. Jeff opened the rear door, but he paused without going out. Jade stood behind him, bracing her hands on his shoulders and staring out at their sons.

The two were building a snowman. Oblivious to their audience, they were talking.

"No, no! You're packing it all wrong, Sean!"

"Well, don't yell at me!" Sean grumbled back. "I've never done this before!"

Ryan sighed with great patience, like an old man educating a schoolboy.

"You can learn. Quit trying so hard! Have a little patience, and it will come to you."

"Yeah. Yeah, sure," Sean said.

They worked in silence for a while, then Sean suddenly said, "Oh, Ryan, come on ... you're crying again!"

"I ... I can't help it!"

Jade tensed, longing to run out to the little boy, longing to hold him, to try anything to ease his hurt. She started to move; Jeff stopped her.

Sean was already there, sitting down in the snow to hold his stepbrother himself.

"When ... when does it stop hurting so badly?" Ryan sobbed.

Sean was silent for a minute, then he said. "It never stops hurting, Ryan. But it gets a little easier to live with every day. And then somewhere along the line, you start to remember all the good things about someone, and you can even smile when you think about them. It takes a while, though. And I guess that you do have to cry a lot."

"Did you—cry a lot when your dad died?"

"Yeah. A whole, whole lot."

"What do you do to stop?"

Sean hesitated again, thinking. He shrugged. "You do...things. You just keep doing the things you should do. Like dressing and eating and going to school and talking to people and ... building snowmen."

"You make lousy snowmen, Sean."

"I know. And you throw a lousy baseball."

"Hey—"

"I can learn to make a snowman. You can learn to throw a baseball."

Ryan stood up again. He started packing snow, a little fiercely.

Jeff was just about to close the door on the two of them when Ryan spoke again.

"Hey, Sean."

"What?"

"I'm, uh, sorry for the things I said about your mother. I didn't mean them. It was just that...that she wasn't my own, d'you know what I mean?"

"Yeah, I know what you mean. Hey, Ryan. Do you want to know something else I've never done?"

"What?"

A big fat white snowball suddenly went flying into Ryan's face. Sean laughed exultantly. "I've never had a snowball fight!"

"Well, you're going to lose this one!" Ryan returned, and as Jeff closed the door on the boys, Jade was smiling through a mist of tears.

* * *

It was a quiet night. It would take time for Ryan to really be Jade's friend, and she didn't intend to push him. Frieda carried most of the conversation through dinner, though Jeff's dad, a wonderful, dignified, older version of Jeff himself, helped, too. They were wonderful people, warm and welcoming. She was grateful to know them. Somehow, in the midst of tragedy, they had made her feel that she was a real part of the family.

She thought that Jeff would want to be left alone that night; he didn't. He spent some time saying good-night to Ryan, but then he was back in his bedroom with her. He didn't speak at all, he just took her in his arms. He made love to her with a very special tenderness, and for the first time she was certain that he did need her, needed her very much.

They left Chicago the next morning. Frieda was sorry to see them go, and Jeff made her promise to visit them in Florida soon. He thought it would be best for Ryan to get away from the cold and the scene of his mother's funeral.

Ryan did seem much happier at home. In a few days' time, he and Sean were screaming, yelling, shouting, laughing, arguing—being busy little boys and learning to be brothers.

It was good for Jeff and Jade to be home, too. It seemed that the past had been buried in that wind-swept cemetery, leaving them both free to begin life again. Before long they too were laughing, yelling, loving—getting on with living together.

Days passed, weeks . . . months.

And with each moment, their home became a happier one.

It seemed that the culmination of that happiness came as they sat by the dock one afternoon, looking at the new sailboat they had finally bought.

Jeff ruffled her hair against her cheek and drew her down to the grass by the water's edge.

"This is heaven. This is all a man could ever want. We've got a private world here, our home, the breeze, the sun, the bay. I live in Eden—with you."

Jade smiled and drew a finger down his chest.

"It's a fun life, huh?"

"Umm." He settled his head in her lap. "And just think, we can start sailing around. Go to the Bahamas, just take off!"

Jade hesitated. "It might not be quite so easy."

"Why not? The boys are almost ten, big kids. They can help with the work. We'll be as free as birds."

"Uh . . . not exactly."

"And why not?"

"Well, Ryan and Sean are pretty easy. But I don't know. We're going to have to pack scores of diapers, baby food and the like. Vitamins . . . whatever else babies need. Honestly, I don't quite remember."

Jade held her breath, waiting for his reaction. He sat up and lit a cigarette.

"You're nervous!" she accused.

"Yeah, yeah, I'm nervous."

But then he tossed the cigarette out into the bay, whirled around and toppled her back onto the grass.

"A baby?"

"Yes."

"Ours?"

"Jeff!"

"No, no, I didn't mean it that way...I mean, really? Are you sure?"

She didn't know whether to smile or not. "Quite," she said primly.

He started to laugh, and he sounded just like Ryan when he breathed, "Wow!"

"You're...happy?"

"Deliriously!"

"Oh, really, Jeff?"

"Absolutely!"

He kissed her. The kiss began tenderly, but soon it grew very fierce. He broke away from her at last, and when she stared up at him, she wondered about the new child. Sean was so beautiful; Ryan was so beautiful. And this child...this child would be a little like each of them. He or she would be very beautiful, too.

"I love you," Jeff told her huskily. "I love you, and every move you've ever made has made me deliriously happy."

"Oh...Jeff."

He kissed her again. Then he picked her up, and started spinning her around, laughing with pure joy.

"Wow!" he said again, and kissed her. She was dizzy when he released her.

"Wow," she replied softly.

"Oh, wow," he repeated, and he held her close to him, so close that she realized that he wasn't just happy, but also very aroused.

"Jeff!" she warned him. "It's the middle of the day. The middle of Saturday. The boys are in the house!"

"So, my love," he replied, putting his arms over her shoulders and bringing his face to hers. "Let's christen the boat!"

He kissed her again.

"The boat...dinner out somewhere. We'll tell the boys the good news then. But...the boat first."

He moved his hand along her shoulder to her ribs. He stretched it between them, caressing her breast, finding a nipple and quickly bringing it to an erotic peak.

"The boat," she murmured.

Laughing, he caught her hand. They scampered across the grass together; then their feet were clattering on the wooden dock. Breathlessly they gazed at the bay, at the palm trees, reveling in the privacy and serenity of their little jungle.

Then Jeff caught her hand again and they leaped aboard the new sailboat.

Her name was to be the *Genevieve*. Ryan had chosen it.

And that afternoon, with an eternity of tenderness, ferocity, desire and love, the *Genevieve* was duly christened.

Epilogue

Foul ball!" the umpire shrieked.

"You can do it! You can do it, Sean!" There were shrieks from the stands, shrieks from the players not on the field, shrieks from a dozen parents.

Two outs. He had to pitch two outs.

He and Ryan were on the Buccaneers team this year. This was it—the championship game of the season. They were playing the Eagles, and they were in the last inning. The bases were loaded, and if Sean didn't pitch two more outs, the Eagles could undo the present six-five score.

Sean wound up for the pitch. The ball flew.

"Strike two!" the teenage ump yelled.

Sean felt a little dizzy. He could see his mother in the stands, smiling, giving him a thumbs-up sign. Toby was behind the wire, shouting that he knew Sean could do it.

About twenty feet from first base, Jeffrey stood silently watching the field. Arms crossed over his chest, he was handsome and tall, his dark hair tousled, his blue eyes keen as he followed the action.

Whether they won or lost the game, Sean knew, Jeff was going to tell both of them how proud he was. If they won, he'd say, "Super!" If they lost, he would say, "Hey, it's only a game, you know. You played your best, and you played by the rules, and that's all I can ask. Good game, guys, good game."

Sean knew that he was good. He knew that he would play lots of games, and that he would lose some. He was even pretty darned sure that one day he would play in the Major Leagues. He really didn't need his mother's approval, or his stepfather's—not in baseball, anyway. Math . . . well, math was another story.

"Pitcher!" someone yelled.

He wound up and threw the ball.

"Stri—ke three!" the ump called.

Only one more out . . . one more out.

Sean adjusted his cap and stared toward first base. Ryan was there; he could catch with the best of them now. But for some dumb reason, the pitcher always seemed to get the credit for a good game.

His stepbrother smiled at him. "One more, Sean! Just one more!"

Sean nodded and turned back to stare at home plate. The last batter for the Eagles was up. Parents were going crazy all over the place.

"Play ball!" the ump roared.

Sean nodded, but he didn't throw the ball. He dropped it, doubled over and clasped his shoulder, falling to his knees.

He heard his mother scream—darned if he couldn't recognize her scream no matter how much other noise there was—and he gave a quick little prayer that God, and his mom, and his dad up in heaven, would forgive him.

It was his stepfather who reached him first. "Sean? Hey, son, what's wrong. What happened?"

Sean had to look up and hope that his acting would not fail him. "I'm sorry. I'm okay. It's just my shoulder. I guess I got tense and strained it. I'm okay, really."

He saw his mother running up behind Jeff; he saw Jeff wave her away. He saw the concern in her brilliant green eyes, but he saw, too, that she was going to trust Jeff. She forced herself to offer Sean a weak smile, and went back to the stands.

"I'll take you out of the game—" Jeff began.

"No, no. I'm okay. I just think that maybe I'd better not pitch. Switch me—"

"I can't put Tommy back in as pitcher, Sean. He's already played half a game."

"I know. Put Ryan in. He's back-up pitcher."

Sean couldn't read his stepfather's eyes. There were an enigmatic blue.

"I can catch, Jeff. Honest. I just don't think I can pitch."

Jeff hesitated a second. People were clustering around the fences; the Eagles' parents were all whispering excitedly. No one wanted Sean to be hurt, but if he was out as pitcher, they figured they had a sure shot at the game.

"All right, Sean. Switch with Ryan."

Sean nodded. Jeff left the field. Sean went trotting over to first base. "I can't pitch, Ryan. It's your baby."

Panic swept over Ryan's features; he went a little white. His eyes were as big as saucers.

"I can't do it, Sean! I can't! Sean, this is the last guy! If he hits it good, they could win the game!"

"Go, Ryan! You can do it! You got to do it! My shoulder's out!"

He gave Ryan a shove toward the pitching mound. Ryan moved reluctantly.

"Oh, God, please tell me I did the right thing," Sean whispered.

Ryan moved to the mound. Sean was certain that his own team had little faith in their new pitcher, but the parents and the players started rooting for Ryan, anyway. That was the kind of team spirit his step-dad and Toby encouraged: you rooted for whoever was up.

Ryan looked around. He poised himself. He wound up for the pitch.

"Strike one!"

Sean could see the deep breath that Ryan took, then quickly the ball sailed out again.

"Strike two!" the ump screamed.

But then even Sean panicked a bit. The next three pitches were balls. It was two and three. If Ryan blew it again, the player would walk to first. And an Eagle would come home to tie up the score. They would go into extra innings.

"Come on, come on, come on. You can do it," Sean whispered beneath his breath.

There wasn't a sound from the crowd.

Ryan wound up, and the ball flew.

"Strike three!" the ump called.

Wow, Sean thought. It was just like a circus. Parents were screaming their heads off. People were rushing everywhere. The whole team was running toward Ryan.

Toby reached him first and threw him right into the air. The whole team was there, patting him on the back, yelling his name.

Sean shuffled his feet in the dirt and smiled. He realized that someone was standing in front of him and he looked up into his stepfather's sceptical blue eyes.

"How's the shoulder, Sean?"

"What? Oh, I think it's going to be okay. Just a kink, you know."

"Sean, he might not have made it, you know."

"I knew he could! I knew it! He just—" He flushed, aware that he had given himself away. "I...I'm sorry. I guess I really should have been thinking about the whole team. But Jeff, honest to God, I knew that he could do it—and he did!"

Jeff smiled then. He put an arm around Sean's shoulder and led him toward the rest of the team.

"Did I ever tell you, Sean, just how damned proud I am to be your stepfather?"

Sean went a little red. He lowered his head. "Mom would go crazy if she heard you cuss around me or Ryan," he said a little uneasily.

Jeff laughed. "Well, yeah. And she'd be right. But this is one of those real man to man moments, Sean. I was thinking that you were a whole lot older than you are."

Sean felt his eyes get a little teary.

"You sure you're all right, Sean?" Jeff asked.

"Yeah, yeah." Impatiently, Sean brushed at his eyes with the back of his hand. "Come on, let's go! The Eagles have to buy us ice cream!"

They walked toward the fence and the parked cars. Kids and parents were beginning to move away, still yelling and calling out. Sean saw Ryan right away.

Jeff picked up his own son and gave him a great bear hug. "Never got off a sticky one like that quite so well myself!" he said.

Ryan beamed. Even the tips of his ears turned red. He mumbled something happily to his father, hugging him back. Then, over Jeff's shoulder, he saw Sean.

"You did that on purpose!" he mouthed.

"Hey, no, man!" Sean protested.

And then Ryan smiled.

Sean had experienced a few moments of doubt, and a few minutes of envy. It was nice, after all, to be in the limelight. Nice to have everyone yelling and screaming and cheering for him.

But it was all worth it. With that one smile, it was all worth it. Sean had forgiven Ryan a long time ago for the things he'd said about Jade. He knew that Ryan had just been hurt. Hurt, that same kind of bad, want-to-die hurt that he himself had felt when he had lost his father. Maybe that was why it was so great now. All of them—his mom, Jeff, Ryan, and himself—they'd learned what it was like to hurt. And they'd made it, anyway.

"Hey, Slugger, how's the arm?"

Jade, who had been with Ryan, finally reached Sean. He couldn't tell her that he'd made the injury up. But he couldn't leave that worried look in her eyes.

"Must have been a little cramp. It's fine now.

"Really?"

"Yeah."

She bent down next to him. As always, she smelled good, like flowers. Her tawny hair swept over his grubby Buccaneers shirt as she whispered in his ear.

"You're a rotten liar, Sean. You always have been. But I love you to pieces. You're pretty special."

He knew that he had turned red. "Aw, Mom!"

She laughed.

"Let's go!" Jeff called.

"You forgot," she called back. "I've got my own car! I had to wait for the pool cleaner this morning, remember?"

"Oh, yeah," Jeff muttered. He shrugged. "Let's drop the Volvo off at the house. I'll follow you and we'll drive to the ice cream parlor together. I'll take the boys now. Ryan, Sean, hop in the Lincoln."

Jade grinned, gave Sean a little wave and started for the Volvo Jeff had bought her for her birthday. Sean and Ryan went after Jeff. In the back seat of the car, they immediately started rehashing the game.

"I thought we were gonners in the second inning!" Ryan told Sean.

"Yeah, when the new kid whacked the ball into the next field?"

"Yeah, it's a good thing only one guy was on base."

"Luck does have something to do with it sometimes," Jeff said, meeting their eyes in the rearview mirror as he put the car into reverse. "That's something that—"

Crunch!

The sound of bumpers slamming together reverberated through the car. Jeff glared into the rearview mirror and began muttering.

"Dammit! She still can't drive worth beans!"

Sean and Ryan looked at each other, clamped their hands over their mouths and burst into laughter, anyway. Jeff was already out of the car. The boys turned around, kneeling on the seat to stare out the back window.

Jade had her hands on her hips. Her sun-touched hair was flying in the wind and her eyes were bright with anger as she tried to outshout Jeff.

"You chauvinistic twit! You never look where you're going!"

"You wouldn't be a safe driver on a four-lane, one-way road, you ding-a-ling!

"It wasn't my fault—"

"It sure as hell wasn't mine!"

Jeff looked a bit threatening, Sean thought. He was a whole lot taller than Jade, and the way he was leaning toward her was a little bit scary.

But then Sean realized that they had both become silent. They were staring at each other as smiles slowly crept onto their mouths.

Then they burst into laughter. Jeff put his arms around Jade and hugged her, and still they were laughing.

"You're the twit!" Jeff told Jade.

"Uh-uh," she protested. "You really are a temperamental chauvinist."

"I wonder if we'll be doing this all our lives?" he sighed.

"If we are, it will be a small price to pay for spending those lives together."

"A very small price," Jeff agreed, and his lips lowered to hers.

After a moment they became aware that they were not alone. Slightly confused, Jade broke away from Jeff. From the back seat of the Lincoln, Sean and Ryan were applauding. Clustered around the two cars were Toby and Lynn and Miriam and a score of others, all applauding, too.

Jade flushed; Jeffrey grinned wickedly and bowed to them all. "Was that for the entertainment of the fight, or the kiss?" Jeff yelled to Toby.

"Both!" Toby yelled back.

Sean decided that the two of them looked beautiful then. Well, they were beautiful. His mother was, at least. Jeff was handsome. But together...

Yeah, together, beautiful was the right word. They glowed with happiness, and that happiness touched everyone around them.

"I wonder what it will be like with the new baby?" he asked Ryan.

"Smelly, probably," Ryan grimaced.

Sean laughed. "That's not what I meant. It will be strange. He'll really be your brother—and he'll really be my brother."

"If it's a boy."

"Let's be optimistic here, okay?"

"Sure." Then Ryan became serious, too. "It will be neat, 'cause it will kind of bind us all together, you know?"

"He'll be a Martin, though."

"Yeah, well, that's the way they do it. A baby gets his father's last name." He hesitated. "It's your mother's last name, too, you know."

"I know."

"But dad was saying that he always liked the name Daniel; he thought you might like that for a first name. Kind of for your dad, too, in a way."

"Really?" Sean said.

"Really. I wouldn't make something like that up. Honest, I wouldn't."

Sean felt like he was going to cry again. How dumb. He moved quickly to stick his head out the open car door.

"Hey! Could you two please quit necking for a while? We're going to miss the ice cream!"

"Sean!" Jade snapped, but she said a little breathlessly to Jeff, "I think we'd better quit necking."

"For now."

"Are we making a date?"

"You bet."

"Later."

"At the house."

"At the house."

"Tonight."

"Promise?"

"You bet," Jade said huskily. "I don't mess with the Major Leaguers, Mr. Martin."

"You're pretty Major League yourself, lady."

"You think so?"

"I know so."

"I love you."

"I love you, too."

"Mom!"

"Dad!"

"Ice cream!" Jade and Jeff said in unison. And with a last kiss, they broke away from each other with the wonderful assurance that they would never really be far apart. Before too long, night would come with its very personal, very private and special magic.

ATTRACTIVE, SPACE SAVING BOOK RACK

Display your most prized novels on this handsome and sturdy book rack. The hand-rubbed walnut finish will blend into your library decor with quiet elegance, providing a practical organizer for your favorite hard-or soft-covered books.

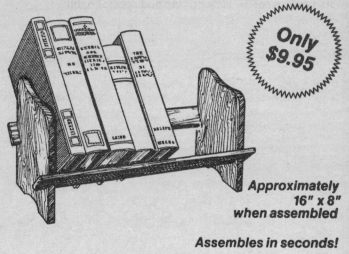

Only $9.95

**Approximately
16" x 8"
when assembled**

Assembles in seconds!

To order, rush your name, address and zip code, along with a check or money order for $10.70 ($9.95 plus 75¢ postage and handling) (New York residents add appropriate sales tax), payable to *Silhouette Reader Service* to:

In the U.S.

Silhouette Reader Service
Book Rack Offer
901 Fuhrmann Blvd.
P.O. Box 1325
Buffalo, NY 14269-1325

Offer not available in Canada.

BKR-2